Me & Mister Everything

By:

Brooke St. James

Other titles available from Brooke St. James:

Another Shot:
(A Modern-Day Ruth and Boaz Story)

When Lightning Strikes

Something of a Storm (All in Good Time #1)
Someone Someday (All in Good Time #2)

Finally My Forever (Meant for Me #1)
Finally My Heart's Desire (Meant for Me #2)
Finally My Happy Ending (Meant for Me #3)

Shot by Cupid's Arrow

Dreams of Us

Meet Me in Myrtle Beach (Hunt Family #1)
Kiss Me in Carolina (Hunt Family #2)
California's Calling (Hunt Family #3)
Back to the Beach (Hunt Family #4)
It's About Time (Hunt Family #5)

Loved Bayou (Martin Family #1)
Dear California (Martin Family #2)
My One Regret (Martin Family #3)
Broken and Beautiful (Martin Family #4)
Back to the Bayou (Martin Family #5)

Almost Christmas

JFK to Dublin (Shower & Shelter Artist Collective #1)
Not Your Average Joe (Shower & Shelter Artist Collective #2)
So Much for Boundaries (Shower & Shelter Artist Collective #3)
Suddenly Starstruck (Shower & Shelter Artist Collective #4)
Love Stung (Shower & Shelter Artist Collective #5)
My American Angel (Shower & Shelter Artist Collective #6)

Summer of '65 (Bishop Family #1)
Jesse's Girl (Bishop Family #2)
Maybe Memphis (Bishop Family #3)
So Happy Together (Bishop Family #4)
My Little Gypsy (Bishop Family #5)
Malibu by Moonlight (Bishop Family #6)
The Harder They Fall (Bishop Family #7)
Come Friday (Bishop Family #8)

So This is Love (Miami Stories #1)

Chapter 1

Olivia Tanner
Philadelphia, Pennsylvania

Some families did not have a black sheep.

I had never done scientific research on the subject or even so much as read an article, but I knew enough real-life families to know that some of them escaped having an oddball sibling.

My father, Benjamin Tanner, was a textbook oddball. He was, no question, the black sheep of the Tanner family. He had extremely successful siblings, but my father could never seem to find his footing. He got stuck in this cycle of taking and then quitting entry-level jobs.

There was also a lot of changing of girlfriends and several near-marriages. He had two children, myself and my half-brother, Jude, but Dad hadn't ever married either of our mothers. He was a lady's man. It was a running joke between Jude and me that there were other siblings we didn't know about. My father had not made the best choices in his life.

Meanwhile, his sister was a banker and his brother was one of the most famous professional basketball players of all time who now owned a hugely successful racehorse farm in Lexington,

Kentucky. My father's siblings had it all together, but our little section of the family was a little less… predictable.

Jude and I never had to actively compare ourselves with our cousins, though, because they lived in Kentucky where my dad was born, and we grew up in Philadelphia. We knew they would do anything for us, but we only saw them once or twice a year.

Our father loved us and everything, but Jude and I had spent a good deal of time with our respective mothers. Jude was a consistent part of my life growing up, but I only got to see him for about five days out of every month when our time with Dad would overlap.

In spite of the fact that he was my half-brother and we spent so much time apart, Jude and I considered one another to be normal siblings. We didn't know any different, so this was a normal sibling relationship to us.

He moved to Lexington to be with our dad's family the summer after he graduated high school, and I hated seeing him go. He didn't even wait for fall. He left the day after his high school graduation. I didn't take it personally or feel like he was leaving me, but he sure did get out of Philadelphia quickly.

I missed Jude, but I wanted the best for him and ultimately wanted him to do what was right for his own future—even if it meant living in the stables with the horses at our uncle's house.

Jude was seriously living in Uncle Ezekiel's stables, which was also something he and I joked about. It was the truth, but it wasn't nearly as rustic as it sounded. Ezekiel gave him a job working with his race horses and also paid his college tuition. He was working as a stable hand and learning about horse breeding and training while getting his degree in engineering. He lived in one of the groom's apartments that was connected to one of their newer stables. It was just a little one-bedroom place, but it was newer and nicer than the apartment I shared with a roommate in Philly.

He had been living there for a few years, so I had been to his apartment several times. Each time, I was more and more convinced that he had done the right thing by taking Uncle Ezekiel up on the offer to pay his tuition. As the years passed, I realized that I had probably made a mistake by rushing into work.

Uncle E would say the offer still stood if I wanted to go to college, but I was settled in Philadelphia. I had friends and had worked my way up to a full-time job at a large advertising firm. The longer I worked, the more I realized that I would have been better prepared for the workforce if I had gone to college first, but I didn't think that it was worth getting off track to go back to school now that I already had momentum.

I also had a job I enjoyed at a coffee shop, but it was only eight hours a week and I did it because I actually had fun being a barista. I worked the front counter and I enjoyed meeting and talking to people over coffee. I only worked two short shifts a week, but I had regulars. Sometimes it felt like I was at my own kitchen and people were coming to visit me.

I liked my jobs and my life. I wasn't even mad that I was on my way to work on Christmas Eve. I was only thinking about all of these things because I had just listened to a message from my brother and I was about to call him back.

He sounded happy and playful on his message, and I smiled as I held the phone to my ear, waiting for him to pick up. Most of the time, we kept in touch via texts, but sometimes he'd call just to talk. Usually, he told me about his girlfriends (he had just broken up with one), his school, or his job. And I would talk to him about my jobs or friends since I almost never had boyfriends. It didn't surprise me that he had chosen to call today since it was almost Christmas.

"Hey Liv," was how he answered the phone.

Jude was one of only a few people in the whole world who called me Liv.

My father called me Livi, thus our family in Kentucky all called me Livi, but pretty much everyone else in my life called me Olivia.

This included my mother, most of my friends, and my coworkers. I smiled at the sound of my brother saying my name.

"Hey, Jude. Merry Christmas, brother."

"Merry Christmas," he said.

"What are you doing?" I asked.

"I'm at Uncle E's. Jordan's friends from the team are coming over later for lunch. Uncle E's got some meat slow-roasting on the grill, so I'm over here hanging out. What about you?"

"I'm on my way to work."

"Work? Why? On Christmas Eve?"

"Yes. The coffee shop is open today, and I don't mind," I said. "I volunteered."

"I hope you're not working tomorrow."

"I'm not. We're closed. I'm not even normally on the schedule today. I usually work on Thursday evenings and Saturday mornings. I told them I'd do it today. I don't really have anything going on till tomorrow."

"What do you have planned for tomorrow?"

"I'll go to my mom's in the morning and stay through lunch, and then I'll go by Dad's in the afternoon."

"I wish you were coming down here," he said.

I smiled even though he couldn't see me. "I'm coming soon."

"I know. I'm excited. How long are you staying?"

"Five days, I think. It might be six. I have a week's vacation, and I'll be in Kentucky the whole time, basically. Aunt Rhonda sent me my itinerary when she made the reservation, but I haven't looked at it in a while. She planned it around Jordan and

Tanner's basketball games. I think I get to see four or five games while I'm there."

"Are you staying with me or in the big house?"

"You ask me that every time," I said.

"And you always say you're staying in the big house."

"Yep," I said.

"But you always crash on the couch in my apartment."

"Not always," I said.

"Two of the five nights, you're going to end up sleeping at my place."

"Yeah, but that's just because we'll stay up late and I'll be too cold and tired to go back to Uncle E's."

Jude let out a little laugh at that. "I can't wait till you get here. I want to show you this horse I really want to buy," he said. "Mister Everything. He's a yearling."

"You mean you want to personally buy it, or buy it for Uncle E?"

"Me personally."

"Where are you gonna get the money to do that? I thought they were really expensive."

"They are. And that's the problem. I've got a few ideas about where to get the money. I could probably double someone's investment if I could find someone with that much cash. But it's a gamble. I'm not a businessman or a salesman. I don't know what to promise people or what to say if things go wrong.

You know, things happen. Broken legs happen. And lots of other things."

"I'm surprised you don't just ask Uncle E to help you out."

"Do you mean with coaching or with money?"

"Both."

"He's already helping me out enough. He's giving me advice and everything, but in the end, it's about me stepping up and selling myself and the horse to someone. I can't see myself asking him to help me with the money. Especially since it's something he would want."

"What's that mean?" I asked.

"He would buy this horse if I didn't. Anyone would at this price. I've already talked to him about it, but I was vague with the details since I didn't want him to think I was asking him for money. Justin really only offered it to me at that price for helping him and Lindsay out on their farm, and I didn't even want to mention specifics to Uncle E."

"It's Justin's right now?" I asked.

"Yeah. He's a yearling that was born on Justin and Lindsay's farm. I've been helping them out with him. I want him so bad. I asked Uncle E how he would feel if I tried to invest in a horse. I didn't tell him what horse it was how much it cost, but I did mention it to him just to see what he'd say. I would have to use one of his stalls."

"What'd he say?" I asked.

"He agreed to it without even thinking about it. I know he would help me buy it if I asked, I just, well, I don't really want to. It's already a big deal that he'd be letting me use the stall and it's just weird to ask him to help me buy something he would buy for himself."

"How much does it cost?" I asked.

"Thirty thousand."

"What?" I asked. "That's a good deal?"

I sounded amazed, and my brother said, "That's *nothing* for this horse. That's like less than half of what Justin and Lindsay could get for him."

"I wish I could write you a check," I said.

"One day you will be able to," he said. "When you're CEO of your firm."

"That's right," I agreed even though it seemed out of reach since I was on my way to work at a coffee shop. "I just wish it was today."

"It's all right. I'll figure it out. I have some ideas. I'm only telling you because I want you to come meet him."

"Who? The horse?"

"Yeah."

"What color is he?"

"Gray. But he'll be white—mostly white. His name is Mister Everything."

"I heard you say that," I said. "It's a good name. Hey, I'm not far from my work," I added, knowing I was only a block from the building.

"You're walking to work?" he asked.

"Yes."

"Isn't it freezing?"

"Yes, but I'm bundled-up. And it's only about a five-block walk from my apartment. It's not worth taking a cab." I looked around. "I thought it would be a lot busier down here, but there's really no one around."

"Did you say you were going to the coffee shop?"

"Yeah. My other job's closed today."

"All jobs should be closed today," he said.

"Christmas Eve? Nah. I'm only working from nine-to-one anyway."

"Why are you working at a coffee shop at all?"

"I don't have to. I want to. I only work there a few hours a week and I get free coffee. It's in the same building as my other job, so I get to stop and pick up a cup every morning before work."

"Sounds like the life," he said.

"Living the dream," I agreed even though now that I was out in the cold weather, I felt like I'd rather be home watching Netflix.

I put my gloved hand over my face and breathed hot air into it since my nose was starting to get numb. "Did you get your present yet?" I asked, somewhat muffled.

"Not yet. Not that I know of. Did you mail it to the big house or to my apartment?"

"To your apartment. I sent a box to the big house too, but I sent yours to your apartment. It's something from me and something from Dad. I mailed it for him." (I also bought it, but I wasn't going to tell Jude that.)

"No, it hasn't come yet," Jude said.

"Dang. It might not get there till after Christmas. I'm sorry. I doubt mail's running today."

"That's no big deal," he said. "It'll be fun to get something after Christmas. Did you open your stuff?" he asked, knowing Aunt Rhonda's package got to me on time.

"I opened one from Aunt Rhonda. I could tell it was a gift card. Everything else I'm saving till tomorrow."

"Did you give Dad his stuff yet?" Jude asked. "No. It's sitting under my Christmas tree. I'll take it to him when I see him tomorrow. You know he's dating that new woman, right? She'll be there, too."

"Yeah, he told me about her. I didn't think about her being there tomorrow. You're not exchanging gifts and all that with her, are you?"

"I'm giving her a scarf," I said. "It's nice, but it's a re-gift from a secret Santa thing at my other job. I had a similar one, so I just left the tags on and wrapped it again."

"What's her name?" Jude asked.

"Samantha. She goes by Sami."

"Have you ever met her?" Jude asked.

"Yeah. She's nice."

"Is she young?" Jude asked.

"Forties, I think. I'm bad at telling. She's younger than dad, but she's not crazy young. She's not as young as Nina."

"Well, there's that," Jude said.

"Yep. I'm just about to walk into work," I said. I had been standing by the door to finish the conversation, and I was cold.

"Okay. Love you," he said. "Call me tomorrow after you open your gift."

"I will," I said. "Love you, too."

Chapter 2

It was dead in the coffee shop that day. Roxy's Coffee was situated on the first floor of a high-rise on a busy corner of the city, so I expected that it would be business as usual, even on Christmas Eve. I was concerned when I first saw that there were only two of us scheduled to work that morning. But we were so slow that I could have done it by myself.

I was three hours into my four-hour shift when Brandon asked if he could take his lunch break. He was one of the assistant managers, and he was working open to close. His shift was eight hours today instead of four like me.

"I have to get a last-minute gift for a party tonight," he said. "I hate to leave you alone, but I'll be, like, not even a block away if you need anything. I wouldn't ask, but the store closes before I get off work."

"Of course you can go," I said without hesitation. "I'm fine here. You don't need to worry. Take your time. I'll call you if I need anything."

Within moments, Brandon was gone and it was just me and the older gentleman who had been sitting in the corner of the cafe on his laptop for the last two hours.

I was stooped down wiping out the under-the-counter fridge when the door opened. There was a soft dinging sound that came from a speaker behind the counter, and I stood within seconds of hearing it.

"Hello," I said as I came out from behind the counter and saw that someone was heading my way.

"Whoa, you're like a jack in the box," the gentleman said, smiling.

I instantly swayed back and forth with my palms in the air, doing my best impression of a Jack who had just popped out of a box. I only did the motion for a second or two, but he must have gotten my joke because his smile broadened.

"Welcome to Roxy's." I said.

"Thank you," he said.

There was a row of barstools on the other side of the counter close to where I was standing, and the gentleman headed that way. I gestured toward the register and almost mentioned that he should meet me over there if he wanted to place an order, but I held my tongue. He was incredibly good looking and he seemed so confident and relaxed that I felt compelled to just stand there and watch him cross to a stool and take a seat on it. I figured there was no harm in taking his order from right there if he wanted anything.

But maybe he didn't want anything.

Maybe he was waiting on someone.

Probably his wife.

He was definitely married.

He had a casual appearance, but he smelled nice and his clothes were wrinkle-free.

My friend from high school, Amanda Carol, told me that *if a guy's clothes have wrinkles, that means he's single.* She said only a man's mother or his wife would make sure his clothes were straight. She said it was a sure-fire way to tell. There were, no doubt, exceptions to that rule, but by and large, I trusted it. I had seen it in my own life that even men with good hygiene were likely to look over this aspect of self-grooming.

This guy's clothes, while casual, were well-fitted and completely void of wrinkles. I wouldn't have normally looked for a wedding ring within the first minute of meeting someone, but I was curious enough about the wrinkles that I did with him.

He was roughly my age—mid to late twenties, and his hair was brown at the root with bits of honey blonde on the tips. It was a little shaggy, too. It wasn't long enough to put into a ponytail, but it was long enough to be messily brushed away from his face. He could have passed for someone who just came off of the beach, not someone who just walked in from the freezing cold and took off his hat and coat.

There was no other way to put it than to say that he was hot. He was hotter than hot. His face was basically perfect—the stuff of A-list actors. He had piercing green eyes and a certain magnetism about him that made me think I had seen him before. I wondered if he was famous. He was young and handsome, and so obviously wrinkle-free and married.

I inspected his hand, which had no ring.

It was an uncommon thing for me to look down at a man's hand, and I got nervous about it. I smiled and began talking. "It's cold out there, huh?" I said. And then I added, "Let me know if you'd like to order something."

I began rinsing the towel I had been using in the fridge, and I focused my attention on that instead of the guy.

"I'll have something warm," he said.

"Coffee or tea?" I asked. "Hot chocolate?"

"Coffee," he said. "And some food. A sandwich."

"The ham and cheese?" I asked.

"Sure. Is it the special or something?"

"No, it's just my favorite."

He smiled. "That sounds good."

"Would you like a cup of house coffee, or an espresso drink?"

"Either," he said. "Whatever you feel like making."

"If you let me choose, I'll probably pick something more complicated than house coffee." I patted the espresso machine. "I haven't made many drinks today. I'm missing my old friend."

He laughed. "Yeah, I see you're not very busy. You probably shouldn't even be working today."

"Oh, I don't mind," I said, smiling as I headed for the kitchen. "I'll be right back. Let me get this ham and cheese started for you."

All of our food was prepped so there was little to no actual cooking. Whoever prepped it used quality ingredients, but all I had to do was put on a glove, take it out of a container that was in the fridge and put it through this toaster on a conveyer belt. It would come out warm and ready to eat on the other side. I had the thought that I was going to make myself one just like it to eat for lunch when I got off work.

I went back to the counter after what must have been only thirty seconds. "That was fast."

"All I had to do was talk to the chef," I said.

"And by *talk to the chef* you mean toss a sandwich into the toaster," he said.

"Yes," I said, laughing. "That's exactly what I mean. So, you've obviously been here before."

"I have and I love that ham and cheese. I get it all the time."

"I do too," I said. "I was just promising myself that I'd have one when I get off work."

"When's that?" he asked.

"In an hour," I said. "Maybe forty-five minutes. One o'clock."

"Could I get you to put another one through the toaster for me?" he asked.

"Did you want two?" I asked, wondering based on our conversation, if he intended to give me the second one. That couldn't possibly be true, though.

"Yeah, I'll take two," he said.

"Sure thing," I agreed. "Let me run back and get that started."

I turned on my heel and went into the small kitchen area again. I quickly went through the motions of gloving up, taking a second sandwich out of the fridge, and placing it on the end of the toaster. The first sandwich was about a third of the way through its trip through the toaster. I knew I would have just enough time to make his coffee drink and then come back and get them. I was familiar with the layout of the coffee shop, and again, even with the process of gloving-up, it took me less than a minute to tend to the sandwich and make my way back to the front.

"Okay," I said, dusting my hands on my apron as I opened the swinging door.

"Are you the only one here?" he asked. He was smiling. He wasn't asking because I was giving him bad service. He just seemed curious.

I felt at ease talking to him. "I have help, but he went on break," I said. "Brandon," I added, since the guy had obviously been here before.

He nodded, but I couldn't tell if he recognized the name or not. His green eyes were utterly distracting.

"Your sandwiches will be ready in just a few minutes. Did you still want me to choose a drink for you?" I asked, going to stand in front of the espresso machine.

"I'd love that," he said.

"Any requests, like a certain kind of milk or sugar?"

"If I was ordering, I'd tell you I don't care for it to be overly sweet, but I'm not picky and I like to try new things. Milk doesn't matter, either. I like it with and without. You can't go wrong, honestly. I like everything on the menu."

"Okay," I said. I made a double shot of espresso and sweetened it just a little with raw sugar before steaming whole milk and adding froth to the top. I enjoyed a good cappuccino and I knew how to make one well. I added a sprinkle of raw sugar to the top of the froth before setting it in front of him.

"No flavors or anything," I said. "Just a cappuccino—slightly sweetened."

"Thank you," he said, smiling appreciatively at the cup as I slid it toward him. "This looks great. Do I need to pay you now?"

"I'll go see about your sandwiches," I said. "We can settle up when you're finished eating."

What in heaven's name had come over me? That was not how we normally did it. We were definitely a pay-before-you-eat coffee shop. I had no idea why I was even offering that.

"What if I dine and dash?" he asked.

"If you do that, I guess I'm buying your lunch," I said with a shrug. "Maybe you should do that," I added. "It'd probably make me feel good to buy someone lunch on Christmas."

As I was talking, I made him a cup of ice water to go with his sandwiches and set it on a napkin near his cappuccino. He thanked me for it with a smile and nod.

"How long have you worked here?" he asked, picking up his coffee.

"A year," I said. "But I don't really *work here*, work here. I mean I do, obviously, but it's not my main job. I'm just here a few hours a week."

"What's your main job?" he asked.

"I work upstairs at Stone Lion advertising firm. I'm a digital artist. I do all kinds of art, but there it's mostly digital. Graphic design, things like that. They do all sorts of stuff up there."

"I know the place," he said with a nod. "Twelfth floor."

I nodded. "You must work in this building too," I said. I felt like I had seen him before.

"Yeah," he agreed just before taking another sip of his coffee.

Just then, the door opened. A dinging sound happened and he and I both glanced that way to see that someone was walking inside. I recognized the people and I smiled at them. It was Christine and her young daughter Sophie. They were my regular customers who came in almost every Saturday morning on their way to the library.

"What's up you pretty ladies?" I asked when I saw who it was.

The man at the bar turned to me when I said that, and I glanced his way. He was stunningly handsome, but I couldn't let myself get distracted.

"Let me run to the back and get your sandwiches," I said. "I'll be right back." I turned to head toward the kitchen again. "I'll meet you girls at the register in just a second," I yelled to Christine from over my shoulder.

Again, it only took a minute to tend to his sandwiches. I served both of them on one large plate. I cut them twice diagonally, making triangles which I arranged into a circular shape that resembled a flower or a sun. I worked quickly and made it out there in no time.

I set the plate in front of the good-looking guy. "I'll go take their order unless you need anything else," I told him.

"This looks great," he said. "Thank you."

I smiled at him and walked over to talk to Christine and Sophie.

"Merry Christmas!" I said in an animated way as I went around the espresso machine and saw the mother/daughter duo.

Turns out, they had come there for me. They brought a tin of cookies and a beautiful Christmas card with personal drawings Sophia had done. It was a thoughtful and unexpected gift.

I made their regular orders—a tea for mom and a hot chocolate for Sophie. I had a conversation with them that lasted somewhere between five and ten minutes. It wasn't customary for us to check on or follow up with the people who were eating in our restaurant, but I glanced at the gentleman occasionally to make sure he was still enjoying his lunch, which he was.

I was so touched by Christine and Sophie's kind gesture that I ended up giving Sophie my favorite lucky cup.

Lucky cups were something I made up.

I was the type of artist who loved pen and ink drawings and who loved to draw on unexpected objects. Paper coffee cups turned out to be a fun medium for me, and I often drew on them. I took cups from Roxy's and worked on them during down time at home or at my other job, and I brought one of the newly decorated ones with me almost every time I worked a shift. I would slip them onto the outside of a cup of coffee and give them away to one lucky customer. Sometimes, I altered the logo in a funny clever way and sometimes I just drew a random scene or character. Most of the time, people would react to it, but every now and then a cup got thrown away without people even knowing they had received something special.

I had a small size cup with a masterpiece drawn on it sitting behind the counter. It had been there for weeks because Belinda, our manager, saw it, loved it, and set it there. That one had taken me hours to draw where most of them took far less time than that. But I grabbed the special one from its spot on the counter and put it on the outside of Sophie's cup. She had drawn me a beautiful picture of us at the coffee shop, and I felt the need to respond.

She and her mother both reacted to it. They knew the concept of a lucky cup. I had given Sophie one of them before and explained it to them. They loved the special one and talked about it being a "double-lucky" and things like that.

We were all smiling as they left.

Chapter 3

After Christine and Sophie left, I walked over to the gentleman who was still working on his ham and cheese sandwiches.

"What just happened?" he asked sitting up and dusting off his hands as he regarded me.

"That was my friend Sophia and her mom," I said.

He smiled skeptically like I was eluding his question, but I wasn't sure what he was asking. I stood in front of him and opened the tin of cookies.

"I think we have to try these. Look what they brought. Don't they look delicious?" I held it out for him to inspect.

He glanced inside and then at me. "Are you sharing?" he asked.

"Yes," I said. "That would be mean of me to show them to you and not offer you one."

He reached inside and took one of the cookies. "Aren't you going to have one?" he asked when he saw me put the lid back on.

"I will when I get off," I said. "I'll have more than one," I added making a face that made him smile.

He took a bite of it, eating over half of it at one time and making a chesty groan of approval as he chewed.

"Good?" I asked.

He nodded and finished chewing before eating the remainder of the cookie. "So good, thank you. I was asking you earlier what happened with you and that little girl. I heard you guys talking about some kind of special cup. I think I heard Belinda mention that one time."

I had no idea when or why Belinda would have ever mentioned my lucky cups to a customer, but I didn't take time to think about it.

"Oh, it's just something I do when I'm working sometimes. I doodle drawings on a cup and give it away. I like to tell people they're *lucky cups* so they feel special for getting one."

"That's fun," he said, staring at me. "I wish I'd get a lucky cup."

"Aw, shoot. I had one this morning that I gave to a guy who didn't even notice it, and that one I gave to Sophie just now was one I did a while back. If I see you come in sometime when I'm working again, I'll hook you up. I could whip one up right now, but it wouldn't be as good as if I took my time."

"Are you the only one who does it?" he asked.

"Yeah," I said. I was confident at first, and then I reconsidered. "I think so," I amended. "I know I started it, but maybe someone else is doing it if Belinda mentioned it to you. I don't really work here enough to know."

"What's your name?" he asked.

"Olivia," I said.

He was no longer eating, but he didn't seem to be in a hurry to leave. He just leaned back on a barstool like he was going to sit there and talk to me.

Feeling a little shy, I went to work absentmindedly wiping things.

"What's your name?" I asked after a moment.

"Eric."

I gave him a nod as I glanced at him, thinking he looked like an Eric. "Are you having a good Christmas so far?" I asked since I was a big dork and I didn't know what else to say.

"I am. I've been traveling for almost a month, so it's good to be home."

"Oh, wow, where'd you go?" I asked.

"All over. I went to Spain and France and then, most recently, I was in Costa Rica."

"Whoa, you weren't kidding," I said. "I've never been anywhere. Not like that. Kentucky's about as far as I go."

He chuckled at that, and I laughed right along with him since it was pretty random of me to use Kentucky as a boundary.

"I have family in Kentucky," I explained. "That's where my dad grew up."

"Oh, I see," he said, nodding. "I was trying to remember. I don't think I've ever been to Kentucky. I've been to Tennessee. Nashville, for sure."

"Then you probably drove through Kentucky."

"No, I flew."

"Well, then maybe you've never been there."

"I don't think I have," he said.

"I'm going in a couple of weeks," I said. "My brother's living down there while he goes to college, so I'm going to visit him and the rest of my family. My cousins play basketball, so I'll get to see a few games."

"That'll be fun," he said. "Taking a break from your job at Stone Lion. You said you were a digital artist, but what is it you do up there? Graphic design?"

"Well, not yet. I'm working my way up. My first love is designing logos and doing product branding. Right now, I basically just draw little elements of designs for my bosses. They have big accounts, and I make royalty free drawings for them to use in their designs. One day, I'll be the one with the big accounts, but for now... I'm a grunt, basically. I'm learning the ropes."

"And you make lucky cups at a coffee shop twice a week," he added.

I smiled and nodded thoughtfully, still wiping things.

"What would you do for a product that was coming from Costa Rica?" he asked.

"What's that mean?" I asked, having no idea what he was saying.

"What kind of logo would you design for a product that came from Costa Rica? How would you brand that?"

"It depends on the product."

"It doesn't matter what the product is. I just wanted something to represent Costa Rica."

"Oh, it's for you?" I asked.

He nodded.

"What's the product?" I asked.

"Something everybody needs."

"Food?" I asked.

"They don't need it quite that much," he said.

"Banana juice? Blankets?"

He laughed. "No. They need this more than banana juice, and maybe more than blankets. At least I do."

"Coffee?" I asked.

He nodded. "How'd you know?"

"You're selling coffee?" I asked.

He nodded again. "From Costa Rica."

"Are you moving there?" I asked.

"No."

"Hmm. So, you're talking about a logo to represent coffee that comes from Costa Rica, but you're going to sell it here?"

"Yes," he said. "You know how the different coffees have their own logo." He pointed to a shelf that displayed all of our shop's different varieties and roasts.

"I would probably just make it round and all-one-color, like a stamp with a simple coastal scene and sunset. I'd have to look up some things and get inspired, but I can hook you up with something cool to represent Costa Rica. That'd be fun."

"Have you done any of the logos of the ones that are up here?" he asked.

"No, but my firm does work with Roxy's. So, I'm sure I did little elements of a lot of this."

"Do you think they've done a good job with the looks of everything? Is there anything you would change?"

I gave him a smile. "Yes, and yes," I said. "Although, I feel like that's a trick question since technically it's my bosses who design this stuff."

"What would you do differently?" he asked.

I shook my head and smiled. "This feels like a trap," I said.

"It's not, I promise. I just seriously want to know. I'm curious."

I reached out and turned a little bag of coffee that was sitting on the counter, situating it where we both could see the logo. It was "Winterbrew" coffee and it featured a design of a cartoon guy in a festive indoor scene.

"His arm is technically on backward," I said. "Most people wouldn't notice but you can see which way the thumb is facing. Also, I think the font could be about half the size on this one. But it's good. I'm not saying these are bad. I think all the execs at Stone Lion do a great job. I really like that firm, or I wouldn't be working there." I shrugged. "But they're really expensive. If you're just starting out and you're looking for a custom logo, I could do a good job and create a logo that represents Costa Rica. I could come up with something for you at barista prices."

"Would you do that?" he asked. "Some freelance work?"

"Sure, definitely," I said. My wheels were already turning, thinking of a design.

"Could I just go through your firm and ask for you?" he asked. "That way you'd get paid to do it at work?"

I shrugged. "If you want to… but that's what I was saying… I could do it for a fraction of the price from my apartment."

I shrugged, feeling my cheeks go pink. I did not expect this conversation to happen, and I did not have enough confidence as an ad designer yet. I hadn't done this enough that I felt comfortable taking jobs and marketing myself. It was because of this sudden rush of nerves that I kept talking.

"You can obviously do whatever you want, though," I said. "You don't have to hire me just because we talked about it. I mean, I didn't even assume you would want to hire me. I was just offering. I could just draw what I was thinking about for free and see if you even like it or not."

I clamped my mouth shut, trying to keep my face from shifting as I cringed inwardly at myself and my ramblings.

"That cookie was really good," Eric said, seeming to ignore my rant.

"Would you like another one?" I asked, thankful for the change of subject.

"I would, but I shouldn't."

"Sure, you should," I said, opening the box again. "It's Christmas."

I held the box in front of him and he stared into it longingly. "They're yours, though, and you don't have a lot."

I shifted the box so that I could stare inside. "Yes, I do. There's got to be at least a dozen in here." I held the box in his direction and gave it a little shake. "If you want one, take it," I said. "It makes me feel good to share."

He hesitated, but only for a second before reaching into the box. "Thank you," he said.

"Merry Christmas," I added.

He smiled as he leaned back and took a bite of the cookie. This time he only ate about a quarter of it on the first bite.

"This is for you, by the way. I didn't touch them." He gestured to the plate—to the remainder of the sandwiches. Three of the triangles still remained on the plate, untouched.

"I ordered that second one for you earlier, and I didn't get to tell you because those customers came in. I wanted you to come sit and eat with me."

"Oh, gosh, that's sweet, you didn't have to..." I hesitated, staring at the plate. I had cut the sandwiches twice. There had been eight triangles on the plate and now there were three. "Wait a minute, you said you ordered me a sandwich," I said.

"I did."

I tilted my head. "It looks like some of it's missing."

He grinned and touched his stomach. "I was hoping you wouldn't notice that. I tried to strategically eat the right ones where it would look like a whole sandwich was left." He paused and nudged his chin at me. "Plus, I'm bigger than you. I figured these were fair portions considering that."

I laughed as I stashed the plate under the counter. "I seriously will eat the rest of this if you're done with it," I said.

"Are you going to eat it later?" he asked.

"Yeah. Once I get off work. It's only like thirty minutes from now."

"And then you're going to a Christmas party?" he asked, even though we hadn't discussed that.

"I might go to one with my friend," I said. "Not a party, but a family get-together."

"Do you have family in town?"

"I do, but my family doesn't have anything going on until tomorrow."

He nodded.

"What about you?" I asked.

"It'll be quiet at our house. I just got back from my trip last night, and my dad just got out of the hospital."

"Oh, why?"

"He was having some chest pains. The doctors said it was a minor heart attack."

"I'm sorry," I said.

"It's okay. He's fine now. He's already home. He'll be eating his weight in lamb and roast duck by this time tomorrow."

"Lamb and roast duck, ay," I said, eyebrows raised and smiling. I thought he had been kidding, but he didn't smile.

"Seriously? Does your family really cook that?"

"Yes. What do you eat for Christmas dinner?"

"My mom makes turkey and stuffing, and maybe a casserole. My dad gets a family pack of stuff from the deli at the grocery store. Most of the time, it's fried chicken and mashed potatoes. It tastes good, but it's definitely nothing as fancy as lamb or duck. I may have never even had those two things separately, but certainly never in the same meal."

"My family has this lady from France who cooks. She does a huge spread for all the holidays."

"Yeah, that's cool. A French chef. Does she live at your house or something?"

I was half-joking, but he nodded and said, "At my parents' house."

"Really?" I asked. "She *lives* there?"

He nodded as he sat back on his stool and crossed his arms. I tried not to seem that impressed or disbelieving, but I'd never met anyone who had a live-in cook. I didn't even know those existed, even for rich people. My uncle was rich and famous, and he didn't have a live-in cook. I thought this guy was probably teasing me, but I didn't say anything else about it.

"Are you exchanging gifts with anybody for Christmas?" I asked after a few seconds of silence.

"A few people," he said. "I think I bought gifts for ten or twelve people in my life. That's what I'm down here doing now—getting a couple of last-minute ones. How about you?"

"Same," I said, nodding. "Roughly ten or so if I had to guess."

"What about you?" he asked.

I made a confused expression. "What do you mean?"

"What's on your Christmas list? If the sky's the limit?"

"If the sky's the limit, thirty thousand dollars," I said. I laughed. "But realistically, I'm hoping to get a nice throw blanket. Perhaps some new underwear and face lotion."

"Sounds practical," he said. "But why did you say thirty thousand dollars?"

"I was just joking because you said the sky's the limit."

"Yeah, but why didn't you say forty or fifty? Why'd you stop at thirty?"

"Oh, because that's how much I need. Not for me. It's for my brother."

"Is he sick or something?" Eric asked.

"No. Thank goodness. No. Nothing like that. You were asking about Christmas gifts, and I had just talked to him, so... it's a horse he wants. A business investment my brother wants to make. He's a horse guy. He works in Kentucky on my uncle's farm, raising racehorses. My family is all into it. It's this yearling my cousin is selling. I was telling him that I wish I could help him buy it." I smiled and tilted my head at him. "Basically, I want to buy my baby brother a pony for Christmas." I let out a little laugh at how silly it all sounded. "But for real, I like getting the face lotion and all that practical stuff from my parents. It's all stuff I'd need to buy for myself, anyway. What about you? Is Santa bringing you something? A ticket back to Costa Rica, maybe?"

Chapter 4

Eric Strauss

Olivia.

Something was different about her.

She had a spark—something that made Eric curious from the moment he came into the coffee shop. It was his coffee shop, of course—one of six locations all over the city. This particular store wasn't the first, it wasn't the largest, and it wasn't the one Eric spent the most time in. He just happened to go by there because he was in this neighborhood getting a few last-minute Christmas gifts.

He had already heard of this girl, Olivia. He had never met her before today, but Belinda, the store manager of this location, had told him about the lucky cup thing, and he wondered what sort of part-timer would come up with something like that. He liked her from the start, before he ever knew she was the lucky cup girl. He bought her a sandwich and wished that she could've sat down and ate it with him.

He was naturally comfortable around Olivia—drawn to her. She was funny, and cute, and nervous, and she had no idea who Eric was. Even after he told her he wanted her to design a logo for coffee, she didn't seem to put the pieces together. Either that, or she knew exactly who he was and didn't care.

Eric had started this chain of coffee shops eight years ago. Because of his father, Eric had basically unlimited financial backing to get his business started, but he had a good vision and a good team of people working for him, and the small franchise was now making money hand over fist. He named it Roxy's after a sheepdog he had as a child.

This girl, Olivia, didn't seem to have a clue that this was Eric's coffee shop. This also meant that she didn't know his father basically owned half of Philadelphia. He found that he kind of liked it that way. As they talked, he caught himself feeling like he wanted to get involved in her life.

First, he started scheming a way to help her at her job with Stone Lion, and then out of nowhere, at one mention of it from Olivia, he started considering investing in a racehorse.

Honestly, the first thing that crossed his mind when Olivia said she needed thirty thousand dollars was to give it to her, no questions asked. Eric had never given away an amount quite so high, but he did like to do spontaneous things with money, and he almost offered it to her on the spot.

But then he thought about it and he realized it might be fun to own a racehorse. Plus, it would give him an opportunity to talk to Olivia again. Eric knew that the selfless thing to do would be to give it to her with no strings attached and call it a day. But he stared at her, feeling like he wanted to have an excuse to run into her again. He told himself that giving a gift of that magnitude to a beautiful, young, dark haired, dark eyed woman would raise eyebrows. He told himself that he wasn't being selfish when he said, "I might want to talk to you about buying that horse."

Olivia had been talking about Christmas, and she just asked him what he was getting for Christmas, so his statement made it sound like a horse was on his Christmas list. She tilted her head at him curiously and he shrugged.

"You were saying your brother had a horse for sale, and I was just thinking… since I didn't get myself anything for Christmas."

She let out a laugh. "That would be amazing," she said lightheartedly, as if he was surely joking.

"What do I have to do?" he asked, staring at her. "Who should I talk to? Your brother?"

Her expression changed as she stared at him, trying to gauge if he was serious.

"It's a ton of money, and it's not like you get a horse to come live with you. It's just like—investing in my brother's horse or whatever. It wouldn't be, you know, a horse that you get to keep."

He gave her a slow grin.

She was adorable.

"Thank goodness it's not a horse I can keep," he said. "I don't know the first thing about horses. I know what it means to invest in a racehorse, though."

"And don't forget about the money."

"I didn't."

"It's a lot."

"I know."

"Thirty thousand," she said.

"Okay."

"Can you seriously get that much?" she asked, her eyebrows furrowed.

"Yes," he said, deadpan.

"And you would have interest in investing in a horse? Because my brother would *definitely* want to talk to you about it."

"Okay, well, let's talk," Eric said with a casual shrug. "I would love to talk to your brother about it."

He didn't care what the investment was. He didn't care if he got a return on it or not. He was going to do it no matter what. In his mind, the money was hers.

"This is amazing," she said, glancing around and looking awestruck. "I feel like this is some kind a Christmas miracle right now. Jude is going to *freak out* when I tell him. But don't feel like you have to… I won't tell him you're for sure going to do it. I'll just tell him you want to talk to him about it. I don't know enough about it to tell you exactly what's going on. I'm sure you'll want to check it out or whatever."

Eric didn't care what it was. But he didn't feel like he should come out and say that. Instead, he smiled and nodded. Olivia was so excited that she reached up and touched her chest. Eric watched as her delicate hand came to rest on her chest, over her heart, like she was feeling for a pulse. Her nails were painted red and green in an alternating pattern. Her nails were shorter and natural with no layers of acrylic or fancy French manicure. The nail polish was chipping around some of the edges. Eric had the passing thought that none of the other women he dated (and he had dated quite a few) would ever have nails that looked like that. He could just imagine her at home painting every other one green and red.

"My heart's beating like crazy," she said, her hand still resting on her chest.

His was too.

"It would be the craziest kind of miracle if it actually works out where you want to do this."

"I do want to do it," he said. "There's nothing to work out. Just put me in touch with your brother."

Eric knew this sort of gesture would come as a shock to other people, but to Eric this amount of money was more like a few hundred dollars. So, in that perspective, the gesture wasn't all that grand. He was excited about the possibility of investing in a racehorse.

Olivia took a paper cup from the counter near the espresso machine and began looking around.

"I'm looking for a pen," she said. "I'm going to write down my brother's cell so you can call and talk to him. His name's Jude. You'll like him, and he knows his stuff with horses. He'll be able to tell you all about it. I wouldn't tell you to do this if I thought he would steer you wrong. It's Jude's first horse, but my family really knows what they're doing, and they'll help him. Nobody's going to try to scam you or anything."

Eric appreciated the reassurance, but really, he didn't care. It would be nice if things worked out and he ended up breaking even or making some money out of the deal, but honestly, this was not about that.

"So, has your family been breeding horses for a while?" he asked, watching her as she searched absentmindedly behind the counter.

"Yeah. My dad's brother. He's really successful at it. Jude lives down there with him in Kentucky on his farm. It's a huge operation. They know what they're doing. Our cousin and his wife have a farm, too. It's my cousin, Justin, who wants to sell the horse to Jude. I don't guess I can promise anything, but Jude's excited about it. Uhhhh, I can't find a pen anywhere. Hang on just a second. I'll be right back."

She took off toward the kitchen, holding the cup while also remembering to take the plate with the leftover sandwich.

There were plenty of pens in a mug that rested on a shelf right inside the kitchen door, and Olivia held the door open with her foot as she reached for one of them. She set the sandwich down nearby, and in those seconds while her back was turned to Eric, she hatched a plan to draw something cool and make him a spur-of-the-moment lucky cup. It would be the first and only shift she had worked where three lucky cups had been given away.

The bell dinged, and Eric looked over his shoulder to see a guy walk in the door. It was someone he recognized who worked at Roxy's. He had met most or all of the store managers at a company party recently and he had talked to this guy.

"If you don't mind waiting just a moment, I'll write down my brother's information and be right back." Olivia was talking to Eric, and he turned to her and nodded.

"That's fine," he said. "I'll wait."

She waved at Brandon and put one finger in the air letting him know she'd be back in just a minute. He was drawing nearer when she gestured to him, and she figured he'd come that way and meet her in the back.

Brandon didn't realize who Eric was right away. He had been clean-shaven and his hair was combed back when they met, and now his facial hair grew in scruffy patches on his face. Today, he looked like the Hollywood version of a beach bum. Brandon wanted to be friends with this guy. It was no wonder that Roxy's was such a cool place with an owner like him. Eric Strauss was the essence of cool. Brandon wondered how long the owner had been sitting there and whether or not he was upset that Olivia was alone. Both Eric and Olivia had smiled at him when he came inside, so Brandon thought everything must be okay.

Eric didn't care at all that Olivia was working alone. He didn't even think twice about it. She was perfectly capable of watching the store on a day like this, and Eric appreciated the rare interaction with an employee who didn't know who he was.

He liked this girl, Olivia. She was cute. He saw her as a woman, make no mistake about that, but she had an innocent cuteness about her that he didn't notice in most women. Precious, maybe was a better word. There was something precious about Olivia. Maybe it was her full lips and rounded nose that gave her a youthful, innocent appearance, but something about her face made him want to shield her, protect her.

In addition to the coffee chain, Eric had several business investments going on, but none of them felt like this one. This one would be made purely on emotion. Eric thought back to the moments in their conversation when Olivia had laughed or smiled. He wanted to see her do it again just to see if he was remembering it correctly.

"…sold out of them twice since then." Brandon had been talking to Eric, but he was lost in thought and didn't catch what he said.

"Sold out of what?" Eric asked.

"Those ornaments. People went nuts for them. They give them with gift cards."

Eric nodded and smiled. "Oh, yeah, those sold real well at all the locations," he said.

"People are collecting them," Brandon said. His voice shook when he spoke. He was nervous, not only because Eric was the owner but also just because he was cool and Brandon wanted to impress him. "Did Olivia already take care of you?" Brandon asked, looking at the counter for clues that Eric had been served.

"She did. I already ate lunch and everything."

"Oh, I, uh, had to go down the block and… I'm working open-to-close today, so I had to use my lunchbreak to do some… I had some last-minute Christmas shopping."

"I hear you," Eric said easily, since he didn't need an excuse. "I'm out here doing the same thing."

Chapter 5

Olivia

I moved quickly.

I didn't even look to see what Brandon was doing. I figured he would either come back here to talk to me in the kitchen, or he would talk to Eric. I was nervous about the possibility of finding an investor for my brother, but my nerves translated into focus, and I concentrated all of my efforts into making a good drawing fast. Or maybe I was making a fast drawing good. Either way, I was rushing but also trying my best.

Horses had always been difficult for me, so I went to Google on my phone and found a reference photo of a racehorse at the finish line. I made an outline, and then I traced the outline ten or twenty times, moving off of the original line here and there to change the shape and give the drawing an intentionally messy look. I added more sweeping curved lines in the tail and mane and filled in the darker details of its eyes, ears, knees, and hooves. I held the cup back, taking in the shape of it and the overall look of my drawing. I added small details like some small piles of dirt on the ground. In perfect block print, I wrote my name and number and also my brother's. I incorporated the handwriting into the drawing of the horse so that the whole thing, including the numbers, looked like a cohesive design—a sticker—a logo. It took me about five minutes to get it where I liked it, and I was working quickly.

I loved the overall look of it. I could have taken a lot longer and made it better, but it was pretty good for an on-the-spot job like this one. I was happy with it and even proud of it as I headed toward the front, but my confidence felt more and more shaken with every step.

Brandon was clearly talking to Eric at the bar, and I didn't feel right about just walking up to him and handing him the cup in front of Brandon. I wondered if I could somehow get the cup to Eric without Brandon noticing me. I didn't think it was possible.

But my momentum was already carrying me that way, and I went to join them, trying my best not to second-guess myself. (There was also the little issue of his unpaid check and my mysterious willingness to eat someone's leftovers.) I realized this whole scene would come as a surprise to Brandon, so I tried to seem really casual and normal.

"Hey Brandon," I said, crossing to the espresso machine. I set the lucky cup on the counter in a strategic place so that it wasn't in Brandon's clear sight. Eric made eye contact with me, and I said, "I'm going to make you a cup of tea for the road."

"Mister Strauss, uh, said y-you took care of his lunch," Brandon said. He was more nervous and awkward than usual.

"I did," I said, assuming Eric was letting me take care of his lunch so that I didn't have to ring him up after the fact in front of my manager. This was more than fine with me considering what he was thinking about doing for my brother.

Brandon let out a nervous laugh as he began doing busywork behind the counter—cleaning the top of the ice bin even though it didn't need it.

"I was telling him the ornaments were a hit this year," Brandon said as he scrubbed away. "Especially the little mugs. Everybody loved those." Brandon smiled and stared at me like I should understand exactly what he was saying, but I honestly had no idea.

"Yeah," I agreed since that seemed appropriate. I nodded and held the smile as I dispensed hot water into a cup. I made Eric a cup of decaffeinated peppermint tea, added a lid, and slid the lucky cup onto the outside of it.

Brandon had already stashed his shopping bag behind the counter. He was still standing there and not looking like he was about to leave us alone, so I decided I had to take action. I set the cup in front of Eric with the drawing facing him and not Brandon.

"I have a few things to do in the back before I clock out," I said. "But it was really nice meeting you. My brother's information is on the cup if you feel like calling him. And, I've got all the..." I gestured to the counter where the sandwich had been, letting him know without saying it out loud that I was planning on paying for his lunch. "Merry Christmas."

I was so nervous that I didn't even give Eric time to respond. I just smiled and turned around, headed for the kitchen again.

"Thank you, Olivia," he called from behind me. I turned and glanced over my shoulder at his words, and he lifted his hand and waved at me. "Thanks for sharing your cookies. And for, everything," he said gesturing the same way I had done. "It was nice meeting you. I'll be in touch with your brother." He spoke quickly, but he seemed serious and sincere, and I gave him a smile and a thankful nod, hoping he would follow through—or at least call my brother and check it out.

I was thinking about the whole encounter moments later as I stared at a spot in the bottom of the sink. There were a ton of dishes, and I had promised Brandon I would take care of them before I left. I hated to leave the handsome stranger, but I was nervous talking to him after Brandon came in, anyway.

In all honesty, Brandon seemed jittery. I had no idea what he was talking about with the whole *ornaments and mug* thing. I remembered it all absentmindedly as I rinsed the dishes clean and loaded them onto the dishwasher tray. I had only been doing that for a few minutes when Brandon opened the door. I glanced that way to find that he was staring at me with wide eyes.

"Did he say anything about me not being here?" was the first thing he asked.

"Who?"

"Eric Strauss," he said. "What are the chances that I would leave you alone for thirty minutes and he would show up? He never comes to our store."

He seemed distressed about it, so I said, "What's the problem? Why does it matter? I was fine."

Brandon shrugged. "I guess it was fine," he said. "If he didn't say anything. I just hate that I wasn't here. Do you think everything was clean enough? Of course, I noticed that display over by the sugar station. Some kid turned all of the granola bars upside down. Do you think he noticed? I'm sure he did, but there's nothing we can do about it now."

Brandon was officially saying the weirdest things I had ever heard him say.

"Is he gone?" I asked.

"Yes," Brandon said with a long sigh.

"I need you to ring me up for some food and drinks once we count out the tip jar," I said.

"I think we only have about twelve dollars each in there," Brandon said.

"Well, I'll just end up putting it into the register," I said. "I probably owe some, too."

"Dang. Somebody's hungry," he said, teasing me since we got half-price food and drinks.

"It's not for me. Not all of it, at least. That guy's lunch and mine. He's thinking about calling my brother to talk about some horse. I told him I would buy his lunch because of that. You know, in the Christmas spirit and everything."

"You told what guy you'd buy his lunch?"

I nodded. "The one you were talking to. Eric."

Brandon laughed. "Oh, you're *buying his lunch*?" he asked, nodding. "How sweet of you." He sounded extremely sarcastic, and I shot him an offended look as I continued to rinse and stack.

"You don't have to ring it up," I said defiantly. "I'll just take it for free if you want me to."

Brandon laughed again.

"What's so funny?" I asked.

"You," he said. "Getting into the Christmas spirit by giving away free meals."

"You don't have to be so jaded about it," I said. "And I wasn't trying to give it away. I was trying to buy it."

"Oh, you're being serious? I—I thought you were joking around," Brandon said.

"I don't know why I would joke about that," I said, still washing and wondering why he was being so weird.

"You must not know who he is."

I glanced at Brandon and he continued.

"Eric Strauss," he said. "The owner and founder of Roxy's."

I swallowed past the lump in my throat. "This Roxy's?" I asked, my voice sounding hoarse.

"Yes, this Roxy's. All the Roxy's. His family owns this whole building, and about twenty other buildings down here. Why do you think there's a big S on the top of it? Strauss Towers, Strauss Arena? Any of this ringing a bell?"

My stomach fell. My face felt flush.

"Are you sure?" I asked. My expression was so confused that it caused Brandon to laugh.

"Yes, I'm sure. That was Eric Strauss, plain as day. Haven't you met him before?" His expression changed to a thoughtful smile as he regarded me. "Did you seriously tell him you were going to buy his lunch?" he asked, looking like he was trying to hold in his laughter.

"Yes," I said. "And he let me do it. He didn't even tell me who he was. He didn't tell me he gets to eat for free. Does he?"

"Of course he does," Brandon said with a disbelieving look on his face. "He can come in here and start hauling the flippin' furniture out if he wants to. He's the owner. He owns everything in this store. His dad owns this whole building. Literally."

I continued to wash dishes as my thoughts began to run wild. The first emotion I processed was excitement for my baby brother. If this guy was as rich as Brandon said he was, then he was probably being serious about investing in the horse. I could not stop a smile from spreading across my face as I thought about that. *What if it worked out for Jude? What were the chances that I would mention that investment to someone who happened to be loaded and capable of doing it?* I would officially be stunned if it worked out.

"Now you see why I was worried about the store? And about not being here. Do you think he felt any sort of way that I wasn't here?"

"No," I said. "He didn't care. He was really nice. I can't believe he didn't tell me who he was, though. I wonder if he would have paid for his food if I didn't offer to buy it for him."

"He probably thought you were just offering to cover it to be funny. He probably thought you knew who he was."

"I don't know," I said, trying to remember our exact conversation. "I'm pretty sure he knew that I thought he was a regular customer."

"He's not, though," Brandon said, being serious.

"Well, now I know that."

"I thought for sure you knew who he was," Brandon said. "With the way you were flirting with him."

"I wasn't flirting," I said, defending myself.

"You made him a lucky cup," Brandon said. "And thought you were buying his lunch. Plus, he was staring at you. You guys were both doing it."

"What? No. I was, we were, my brother has this horse. He wants to buy a horse, and I was talking to him about... we weren't... I wasn't... we already had a whole conversation about other things. Horse things. That's why I made a lucky cup. I was giving him my brother's..."

I sighed as I trailed off, reaching up and using my forearm to get the hair out of my eyes.

"I was putting him in touch with my brother, that's all. I wasn't flirting—at least not because he was the owner. I had no idea who he was."

Chapter 6

I couldn't decide whether or not to call my brother and tell him about Eric. I didn't want him to get his hopes up, but I was excited and I thought there was a real chance that it would work out.

But Jude stood to gain a lot more from this than I did, and I hated to mention it if it wasn't a sure thing. I called him, and even as the phone rang, I couldn't decide whether or not I was going to mention it.

"Twice in one day," was how Jude answered the phone.

There was noise in the background.

"Are you driving?" I asked.

"Yeah, I'm on my way to the stables. One of Jordan's friends wanted a tour. I'm taking him over there to show him around."

"Oh, I'm sorry, is he in the truck with you?"

"No. He's following me. I'll go back to Uncle E's, but he's leaving from the stables."

"I just got done with work, so I was checking in."

"Oh okay, Because I thought you were about to tell me you found someone who wanted to give me thirty thousand for that horse."

"What? Oh, uh…" I let out a little nervous laugh. I hadn't decided whether or not, I was going to tell him about Eric, and the mention of the money made me speechless.

"I'm messing with you," Jude said. "I was just saying that because Aunt Rhonda made me pray earlier."

"What?" I asked.

"Earlier, when I was talking to you on the phone," Jude said. "Aunt Rhonda overheard us talking."

"Oh, goodness."

"I know. And she asked me about it. She asked if it was something she and Uncle E could look at helping me with—you know like giving me a loan or whatever, but I told her I didn't want to do that after everything they..." Jude trailed off. "Anyway, I explained why I hoped to figure it out on my own, and she gave me a big speech about asking God for help and trusting Him and stuff. Then she asked if she could stand there and pray for me—pray for some kind of miracle."

My heart pounded.

I knew that Eric Strauss was my brother's miracle. I was speechless about it, though. I couldn't bring myself to say it out loud. It seemed too unreal.

"You probably will get somebody," I said, my voice shaking. I was on the verge of laughing or crying or both—full of emotion. "I'm sure you will," I added, begging myself not to tell him.

"I know," he said. "And if I don't, it won't be for lack of trying. I already mentioned it to some of guys on the team. Alex Holbrook said he would talk to his dad and see if it's something they'd be interested in."

"I mentioned it to a customer, too," I said, unable to hold it in any longer.

"You did? Who? Where? At the coffee shop?"

"Yeah. Just now. Like thirty minutes ago. He's my boss. I didn't even know it when I was talking to him, though. I told him about it, and I gave him your phone number. He seemed pretty interested."

"What'd you tell him?" Jude asked.

I could instantly hear the hope in his voice, and I cringed, feeling like I needed to make a disclaimer. "I'm sure I didn't tell him enough. And I don't think he knows much about horses. We were talking about Christmas presents, and I mentioned you and this horse you had told me about. I told him I'd buy it for you if I could, and he said he was interested in, you know, investing. I told him a little about you and that you'd be taking care of it, and he seemed to understand. I don't know if anything will come of it, but he did seem interested. He took your number."

"That would be unreal," Jude said. Then he added, "We'll hey, I'm pulling up at the stables."

"Okay, yeah," I said. "Just... his... he might not call right away since it's Christmas and everything."

"Okay, no problem. Yeah, I'll be right there." That last statement was directed toward whoever was waiting for him. I told my brother goodbye and let him get to his business.

It was eight o'clock that evening when Jude called me back.

I was at my roommate's parents' house, but I happened to be holding my phone, taking a picture of her and her dad. I declined the call so that I could snap the photo, and I excused myself and called my brother back within minutes.

"What's up?" I asked when he answered.

"How in the world did you do that?" Jude asked.

"Do what?" I asked, smiling.

"Your friend called me," he said.

"Who?"

"Eric Strauss."

I knew he would say that, but my heart sped up when he actually did.

"He wants in," Jude said, sounding pumped.

"Are you serious?"

"Yes. I can't believe it, but yes. Where are you?"

"Jillian's parents'."

"It's noisy," he said.

"They're playing a game," I said, walking further down the hallway. "What happened with Eric? What did he say?"

"He just introduced himself and told me he had already talked to you about investing in a horse. He was super easy-going. Everything I said, he just agreed with and said it was no problem. You must have done a good job of explaining it to him because he had no problem or questions with anything whatsoever."

"So, did he already agree?"

"Yes. He wants to cover the full amount. He said his bank would be in touch with me and then Justin. It was basically no questions asked. The only questions he asked were the excited ones. *Tell me about the horse. What's his name? What color is he? Do you have a picture you can send?*"

I let out a muffled squeal of excitement. "So, what happens now?" I asked.

"I gave him Justin and Lindsay's number. He's going to work it out with their farm. He said he'll wait until after Christmas but that he would have someone call and take care of it."

"Oh my gosh."

"I know. And I believe him. I like him. We talked for about an hour, and he's cool. I'm stoked to meet him."

"When are you meeting him?"

"I don't know for sure," Jude said. "He did say he wanted to come down here. He mentioned talking to you about that."

"He mentioned talking to me? What did he say?"

"Oh gosh, here we go, Liv."

"What's that mean?" I asked.

"You got all excited just now when I said that, and I could tell he liked you when we were talking on the phone. Are you seeing him or something?"

"No. I told you. I didn't know who he was until today. Why did you say you thought he liked me on the phone? What did he say?"

"I don't know. Nothing specific. I just basically got the feeling he was doing this whole horse transaction for you. And when I told him he should come down here and meet the horse, he mentioned coming with you. He said he was going to talk to you about it."

"Seriously?" I could not stop myself from smiling, and it came across in my voice. "Tell me exactly what he said. Oh, uh, hang on, my uh…"

My phone was ringing.

I could hear a call coming through on the other line, and I held it away from my ear as I was talking to my brother.

"It's… oh snap, Jude, I think it's him. It's a Philadelphia number. It's Eric, I bet. I'll call or text you later."

"Okay, talk to you later, love you, bye," he said in a hurried tone.

"Bye, love you." I pressed the button to switch to the other line. "Hello?" I said, trying to sound normal and unaffected.

"Hello, is this Olivia?"

"It is," I said.

"This is Eric from earlier today at the coffee shop. Is it a bad time?"

"No, no, I'm at a friend's house and they're playing a game, but I'm not in there. I was actually on the phone before you called. I was talking to my brother. He said you called him."

"I did. I like your brother. He's a nice guy. And I'm excited about that horse. I've never thought about doing anything like that before. I'm so glad you mentioned it."

I let out a breath of a laugh. "I'm so glad I mentioned it, too," I said. "You have no idea how glad I am."

A few seconds of silence followed. Eric thought I was going to continue, but I didn't know what to say.

"So, it's really cool that you're doing it," I said.

"I'm excited," he said. "That's why I called you, actually. I know you're at a friend's house so you don't need to answer now, but think about how you would feel if I crash your trip to Lexington for a day or two so I can meet your brother and the horse. I'd like to meet them in person, and I was thinking maybe you could be there to make the introductions."

"Of course. Definitely. I'd love to do that."

I was proud of my family in Kentucky and would love for him to meet them. They were my best chance of impressing him. It was a best-case scenario for him to go to Kentucky. I was grinning from ear to ear at the thought of it when I realized that I must like this guy. I had dated men over the years, and I enjoyed male attention as much as the next woman, but I rarely felt giddy or excited about the possibility of seeing someone again, let alone hoping my family could impress them.

"Okay, well, if you don't mind, send me your itinerary and I'll plan a trip."

"I don't mind at all," I said. "And, do what you want, but a day or two will go fast. There's a lot to do there. You might want to see a couple of basketball games."

"Are you talking about a college game?"

"Yeah. The University of Kentucky."

"You were saying your cousin plays. It's for them, right?"

"Yes. And there's another cousin in high school, too. It's his senior year. He's really good."

"A basketball family," he said.

I had no idea if he knew about Uncle E. I hadn't told him, but I wasn't sure about my brother. "Yeah, big time," I said. "None of my family in Philly play basketball, but all of my Kentucky people do. It's really popular down there."

"I know. UK's always got a good team. That's cool that your cousin plays for them."

"It is cool. It's fun to go to the games and watch him. That's why I was saying you didn't have to hurry back. You know, if you wanted to get, like, the longer tour."

"Okay, I do think I'm interested in the full tour," he said. "Do you think three days would be okay?" he asked. "Is that too long?"

"Oh, definitely not. If anything, it's not enough."

"I'll do three or four, then."

"That sounds great," I said. "I'll check with my aunt about the games and let you know. Send me your email address and I'll send my trip dates and everything."

"Okay, that's perfect," he said.

I really wanted to mention that he could stay at my aunt and uncle's house, but I thought that might be too much.

"Hey, I was serious about you designing something for some Costa Rican beans. That's why I was down there. I had meetings with farmers and ended up making a deal."

"Brandon told me you owned Roxy's," I said.

"I wasn't sure if you knew when we were talking," he said. "I figured you didn't."

"You even told me you wanted that logo for coffee," I said. "I don't know what I was thinking. I didn't even think about it."

"I thought it was cool that you didn't know. I liked seeing how regular customers would get treated."

"I hope I passed the test," I said.

Really, he wasn't normal. He was young and nice and too handsome for his own good. He probably had women buying his lunch all the time— flirting with him when they didn't even know who he was. I didn't say any of that.

"Not that there was one, but I'd say you passed the test. I had fun talking to you and I loved my lucky cup. That was awesome."

"I wish I would have had more time for that," I said. I never liked to admit defeat, but I had to say something. Most of my lucky cups took a half-hour or so. His was okay, but it was nowhere close to as refined as my other ones.

"I wish I could have seen the ones you gave away."

"You can see some of them in pictures. I have given over a hundred of those cups away, and I think about twenty or thirty of them are on Instagram under the hashtag #roxysluckycup. I only work two shifts a week so, it's mostly my regulars or their friends who have posted them. They tag me, that's how I knew about it."

We kept on talking like that for an hour. The time passed in what seemed like seconds. Our conversation flowed effortlessly, and I was so engaged that it startled me when Jillian came around the corner looking for me.

"You okay?" she asked.

I nodded at her. "Hey," I said to Eric. "Can I call you back?" It was an instinctual thing for me to say when I felt like I had to get off of the phone with someone quickly.

"Uh, yeah, you can." There was enough surprise in his voice that I felt the need to backpedal. "I mean, I guess all I need to do is text you the information about my trip, so you can—"

"No, you can call me back, though," he said. "Just call me whenever."

"Okay, I will. Maybe tomorrow or even later tonight."

Jillian was standing there waiting for me, so I was nervous.

"That's fine. I want you to." He said that last part in a reassuring tone, and I smiled.

"Okay I will. I'll talk to you later. Bye."

I called Eric back that evening and we talked for two hours. Then he called me the next evening and we talked again. We talked every day, via text or phone call, for the next two weeks. Christmas came and went, and before I knew it, we were in the middle of January.

Neither of us felt like we were obligated to contact the other one every day, it just always seemed to work out that we got in touch and ended up having a longer conversation than expected.

Eric became my friend. The weird thing was that I couldn't see him as the owner of a successful coffee chain or the heir to his father's fortune. Seeing him in that light made him feel unobtainable, and I didn't want to feel that way, so my brain sort of made a disconnect. The guy I was getting to know on the phone felt like a different guy than the rich business owner. The guy on the phone was simply my new friend Eric.

We talked about music and movies and God and life. We had shared a lot of personal things with each other, but I had kept a few things back, too. I did it intentionally but for no real reason. I didn't tell him that my uncle was Ezekiel Tanner.

He obviously had a few things he wasn't telling me because the day before I left for my trip to Lexington, I got a surprise at work.

My boss called me into his office that afternoon. This wasn't my immediate supervisor, nor was it the one right above her.

This was the Michael. The guy with the corner office. The big boss.

"Come in and have a seat," he said as I walked into his office.

He gestured to the chair across his desk. He stood and shook my hand when I approached his desk and we both took a seat at the same time.

"I have a proposal for you," he said.

"Okay."

"I have to say, I usually don't have these kinds of meetings with junior designers."

I had absolutely no idea what he was about to say.

"You probably already know that one of our clients is Roxy's Coffee," he said.

Eric had called to try to get me on a job. I should have known it. He was always asking how he could help further my career.

"Yes," I said since I knew Roxy's was our client.

"Well the owner of it, Eric Strauss, called me personally this morning. He requested specifically that you, Olivia Tanner, work on a project."

He paused and I nodded with a pleasant but neutral expression. "He would like to do something called a *lucky cup* at all of his Roxy's locations." Michael pronounced the phrase slowly, testing it out.

Again, I nodded, even though I wasn't expecting this.

"You know, Janet's team normally handles our Roxy's account, and I assumed they'd take care of this, but he said he wanted you. He said they were custom, one-of-a-kind pieces and that you were already familiar with them."

"I am familiar with them," I agreed with a nod.

"Good. Their company would like you to produce twelve of these custom pieces a week to be distributed at all of the Roxy's locations."

"Twelve a week for each location or twelve total?" I asked.

"Twelve total," he said.

I nodded.

"We'll still have this go through Janet, so you'll be working with her now. Eric is putting her in touch with his general manager. She'll be contacting you with more detailed instructions. You'll need to get the cups to her so she can make sure they get to the right person. And you'll need to fit it into your work schedule. Free-up some hours. You'll have to pass some of your other duties on to someone else. Get with your current supervisor about that."

I nodded, letting him know I understood.

"I don't know how long something like this takes. I'm not sure what I should tell Janet. Do you know how long they will take you? Is an hour per cup enough? Just make sure she schedules you enough time."

"I will," I said.

"Okay, well, Janet is going to help you get your schedule situated and give you more details. Is this something you'd be interested in doing?" he asked. "I know it's unorthodox, but we'd really like to make this client happy."

"No, it's great, it's good. I would love to do this."

"Good," he said. He smiled at me and tilted his head, staring with a somewhat new appreciation now that Eric Strauss was asking for me by name and willing to pay me to draw on paper cups. "So, I guess you need to email Janet and we'll see about getting you started on this on Monday."

"I'm on vacation next week, but I'll work it out. The owner, Mister Strauss, knows I'll be out of town, so he won't be expecting me to start. I will work it out with Janet, though." I gave him a slight bow. "And thank you. Thank you for the opportunity."

Michael tilted his head again. I had no idea what he was thinking but he was definitely curious about me now. Maybe he was just surprised that I seemed to know Eric. I had a disconnect between my friend Eric and the rich and powerful Eric, and it was weird seeing people look at me as if they were impressed. He was the big boss of my company, and he was sitting there smiling at me curiously. "Where are you going on your vacation?" he asked.

"Lexington, Kentucky."

***

71

"Then, my boss called me into his office and told me they wanted part of my job to be making lucky cups for Roxy's."

I recounted the story to my aunt, uncle, cousins, and brother the following day when we were all having dinner together in Lexington.

Jordan was the only person who lived in the main house with Uncle Ezekiel and Aunt Rhonda, but there were nine of us at their house for dinner that night, and Jordan wasn't even one of them. He was at something for basketball, which wasn't a surprise at all. Jordan was having a great senior season. He was one of the stars of the team, and people were constantly vying for his attention.

My father had two siblings in Kentucky.

Ezekiel, his brother, was the famous one. Ezekiel had two boys, Zeke and Jordan. Zeke was married now, and he and his wife, Allison, were at dinner with us.

My father's sister, Sara, had three kids. Justin, Stella, and Tanner. Justin and his wife, Lindsay also came with their daughter, Piper. There would be times during my trip when more of us would gather, but tonight there were just nine of us. We talked about Stella's spur-of-the moment wedding with a preacher, which had just happened a couple of weeks ago. We ate pasta, bread, and salad, and we sat around the table talking and laughing.

Eric and Jude had talked several times on the phone and Eric had spoken with Justin at least once, so it didn't surprise me that they had questions about him. The whole lucky cup thing at my advertising firm was so new and unexpected that it was one of the first things I brought up to my family when they asked me about Eric.

"And they were the same cups you had been drawing on your own time, anyway?" Uncle E asked.

I nodded, taking a sip of my iced tea. "He's just cool like that. It's not even that he's just doing it because we're friends. He really thinks it's a neat idea and that it'll catch on at the store."

He had told me exactly that same thing the night before when I called to thank him, so I just repeated it to my family.

"So, he's your boss at the coffee shop and he also works with you at your other job?" Aunt Rhonda asked, trying to put all the pieces together.

"I only work at that coffee shop a few hours a week. I do that just for fun and for the discount or whatever. That's the place he owns. Roxy's Coffee. They just happen to use the advertising firm where I work full-time. Eric called my other job and hired me to make those lucky cups for Roxy's."

"And you didn't know he was going to do that?"

"No. My boss just called me into his office yesterday and told me. I talked to Eric plenty before that, and he never mentioned it."

"Has your daddy met him?" Aunt Rhonda asked.

"No, no, no, it's nothing like that."

I knew Eric quite well as a phone acquaintance. But there had been no introducing to family—there had never even been talk of that.

"You'll get to meet him before Ben," Rhonda said, looking at Uncle E.

He nodded.

"Dad might have to give him *the talk*," Zeke said.

"What's that?" I asked feeling nervous.

"You know, the one where a guy gets threatened that he better take care of the lady, or else."

"Oh, no, no, no, that's okay," I said. "He doesn't need the talk. It's not like that. There's no reason for that. We're not, it's not like that between…"

I trailed off, shaking my head and assuming they'd know what I was saying.

"Not like that between what?" Jude asked, teasing me. "You didn't finish your sentence. You talk to him every day. You must be a little interested."

My eyes widened at my brother. I had told him that Eric and I had been talking every day, but I didn't expect him to repeat it in front of everyone.

"Was I not supposed to say that?" he asked, shrugging innocently and causing multiple family members to laugh.

Justin's little girl, Piper, said, "What were you not supposed to say?"

"That Livi's boyfriend's coming to visit," Justin said, answering the question and egging me on the way Jude and all of my cousins did.

I had been around male cousins to know that the best way to evade teasing was to stay calm. I had learned this from years of practice. I smirked and coolly shook my head at Piper.

"He's not my boyfriend," I assured Piper. "He's my boss and my friend, and he's buying a horse from your daddy. He and Jude are."

Piper looked at Jude and he nodded, and I thought I was off the hook. But then she looked at me. "Is he coming to ouw house?"

I nodded, and try as I might, I could not stop myself from blushing. My cheeks turned pink, I knew they did.

"He is," I said, "He's coming to meet everyone and see the horse."

My family, thankfully, did not mention the blushing.

"Did you tell him he's welcome to stay at the house?" Aunt Rhonda asked. "There's an open apartment in the stables since Paul moved."

"What happened to Paul?" I asked, knowing he was Jude's neighbor in the groom's apartments.

"He still works for us," Uncle E said.

"He got married and moved out," Jude added. "Right before Christmas."

"Which means that apartment's vacant," Aunt Rhonda pointed out. "There's no sense in your friend paying for a hotel when we have all this room. It's furnished and everything. There's even towels and toilet paper. It's ready to go if he wants to stay in there."

"I already offered and he said no," Jude said.

Aunt Rhonda leveled me with a stare like she might not trust Jude's persuasion skills. "Make sure he knows how much room we have and that he's welcome," she said.

I nodded. "I will."

Chapter 8

My cousin, Stella, and I had always been close. Physical distance obviously kept us apart for most of our lives, but I saw her once or twice a year for my entire life, and every time, we would just pick up right where we left off.

I was a more open person when I was down here with my Kentucky family. I was still myself, it wasn't that my personality changed, necessarily, it was just that I adopted slightly different mannerisms here than I had in Philly.

For instance, I hugged in Kentucky. None of my Philadelphia friends or family were huggers, not even my mother. So, when I was at home, I wasn't a hugger, either. I maybe gave five or ten hugs a year to people in Philly, and I gave at least that many every day in Kentucky. That was just how my dad's side of the family greeted someone. They sometimes even did it for no other reason than they were standing next to you in a room.

I was always a playful, optimistic person, but in Kentucky, around all of my boy cousins who teased me all the time, I cut up and smack-talked even more. It wasn't that my personality changed, I was just slightly less reserved in Kentucky.

Case in point would be the lip sync battle Stella and I got into that evening while she was at the house getting dressed with me. She came over before Tanner's basketball game to hang out and help me fix my hair. I had been in Lexington for two days, and tonight I would finally see Eric.

Stella and I were so silly and pumped that we danced and sang to a song called *Then He Kissed Me* by the Crystals. We were basically reenacting a scene from a movie called Adventures in Babysitting. We used to watch it all the time when we were kids because it was one of her mother's favorites.

We sang along to that song and danced like we were some serious lip-sync-masters from way back. Stella was freshly married and oh, so in love. And I must have been feeling a little something myself because I acted like a big goof ball, feeling all warm and fuzzy and imagining the whole time that the "he" in the song was Eric.

Stella and I spent an hour or so together before Tanner's basketball game. I didn't gush about it, but she got the idea that I liked Eric. It was hard for me to hide. I was happy, and I was so very anxious to see him. I hadn't seen him since that first day at the coffee shop. I had talked to him a ton since then, but I hadn't seen him in person. It was a surreal feeling, waiting for him, knowing he was coming to Lexington.

I wasn't quite sure how to treat him. We got along so well on the phone, that I wondered if that effortless familiarity would translate to seeing each other in person. I wished I knew if he liked me. I thought he did, but we didn't talk about that or put any sort of label on our budding relationship. It was more of a friendship so far, but I couldn't help but feel like he liked me. I knew I would soon find out.

Stella and I had similar taste in fashion, and she let me wear some of her clothes that night to the game. Her pants were a little tight on me, but I fit into her shirts and we even wore the same size shoe. She wasn't rich, but she had good taste and some nice things, and it was always fun to try on something new. It was cold here. Not quite as cold as it was at home, but I still had to bundle up.

I wore my own jeans but borrowed a shirt/jacket combination from Stella. It was a burgundy shirt with a brown herringbone wool coat. She also let me borrow some brown boots, and we styled my hair down with loose, mermaid waves that Stella made with a curling iron. She brushed it out, making it look natural and beautiful. I loved the whole outfit. I felt put together without looking like I was trying too hard. I was thankful that my cousin had helped me and been willing to share her clothes.

I enjoyed hanging out with Stella so much and missed her when we weren't together. She had been to see me in Philadelphia twice over the years, but my situation there wasn't like their life in Kentucky. My dad had never been as stable as either of his siblings. Stella knew she was welcome to come to Pennsylvania, but we almost always caught up in Lexington.

I felt happy, confident, and full of anticipation that night when we headed to the basketball game. Tanner's game was an 'away game' which meant we traveled to a different high school in town to watch him play. We had seen one of Jordan's games the night before, and I loved the atmosphere at both.

Tanner's high school was huge and they always played in large gymnasiums that were usually crowded, but Jordan's college games were far-and-away a much bigger deal. Last night's game was in a packed arena with jumbotrons, and tonight I had to basically walk on the court with the players to get to our place in the bleachers. It was a large high school, and the gym wasn't tiny or anything, but it definitely wasn't an arena.

There were at least twenty of us in Tanner's cheering section, and I had left them all behind to head toward the front door of the gym. I knew Eric would be there any moment, and I was alive and buzzing with anticipation over it.

I made my way down the bleachers, being careful since I wasn't quite used to Stella's boots. The doors were on the opposite side of the gym. I waited until the players were at the other end of the court to make my exit. I had to walk in front of a bunch of people and then finally behind a few cheerleaders to get through the door.

The next room was full of people but not nearly as crowded as the gym. It was a corridor that led to the restrooms, concessions, and ultimately to the gym entrance. I knew I had time to use the restroom before going out to meet Eric. I had just gotten a text saying that he was on his way from the airport to the gym and the GPS told him he would be here in fifteen minutes.

He was late but it wasn't his fault. He was supposed to arrive at 1pm this afternoon instead of right now, at 6:48pm when we were midway through the first quarter of the game.

There had been weather delays in Philly that set his flight back. He hadn't even checked into his hotel yet. He came straight to the game with his luggage in the back of the rental car.

Eric had a part-time assistant named Alice who took care of his travel plans, and there was always a nice vehicle waiting for him at every airport, no fuss. Sometimes it was a sports car, a sedan, or depending where he was traveling, a truck. This time, it would be an SUV. I knew all of this because he sent me a link to his itinerary and it mentioned the *Range Rover Evoque*. I saw it on the details.

I ran into Stella's new husband, Caleb, near the concessions area. I had been in the bleachers sitting next to Stella the whole time so far, and I knew Caleb hadn't been there. He was in the locker room with the team before they came out, and he was just making his way to the family. I told him where they were sitting, but he seemed like he had done this before, and he was confident he could find them.

He and I ended up talking for a several minutes down there by the concession stand. Stella was my girl, and this trip was my first time to meet her new husband, so I enjoyed getting to know him.

Caleb and I parted ways, and I headed for the door. There were glass doors in front of the gym, so I decided to watch for Eric inside since it was cold out.

I saw that black Range Rover pull into the parking lot, and my heart felt like it was about to explode. It was surreal to me that I was about to see the same guy I had so many conversations with.

You can learn a lot about people through lengthy conversations on the telephone, and I had them almost daily with Eric. It was odd feeling this excited and shaken by someone with whom I had shared so much. Half of me felt entirely comfortable and happy and the other half was nervous and uncertain and full of butterflies.

I resolved to treat Eric like a friend and see where things went from there. I had all sorts of thoughts and made all sorts of plans while I waited for him to park and make his way inside.

I stepped outside once I saw that he was headed my way. I could not help but take in his lean form and athletic looking stride as he walked down the sidewalk that lined the parking lot. It was dark out, but there were plenty of street lights, and he smiled at me when he saw me come outside.

I smiled back, waving at him.

He waved. He was dressed nicely in jeans and boots with a thick thermal shirt layered with a thin coat. He had obviously left his luggage in the truck because he had nothing in his hands. He just walked toward me, his arms barely swinging with his cool stride. I began walking toward him. I felt like I was being drawn to him with an unseen force.

The closer he came to me, the more difficult it was for me to resist. I moved toward him slowly at first, doing my best to keep cool. I had left my purse in the stands with my family, and both of us were open-armed. I blame my impulsive decision to hug him on this convenience and the fact that our momentum was moving toward each other.

I didn't even hesitate when we approached each other. I walked into his arms, and he opened them, taking me in. I let out a relieved sigh, and I smiled because Eric did the same thing—I could hear him and feel his chest expand and contract as he did it.

He smelled nice, and I breathed in the woodsy scent. I couldn't help but notice the feel of his lean muscular body. His embrace gave me a sort of magical feeling, like electricity was coursing through my body. I was pretty sure if you looked at me closely enough I would be glowing. It was a level of excitement and anticipation I had rarely, if ever, experienced. And then I realized that I wasn't sure what he was thinking and maybe this greeting was a little too much. I pulled back smiling but feeling like I had to explain myself.

"I'm sorry. It's Kentucky. They've got me hugging down here," I said as I stepped back.

"Why would you be sorry for that?" he asked lightheartedly, but I was already starting to say something else before he spoke.

"Let's get out of the cold," I said, gesturing toward the gym.

We started walking.

"How was your trip?" I asked, turning to look at him after we fell into stride next to each other on the sidewalk.

"It was good," he said. "Once we got into the air. Did I miss the game?"

"No, no. We're probably in the second quarter," I said. "It had just started a few minutes before you texted me."

We approached the door and Eric reached out to open it for me. Our eyes met as I walked past him, into the gym.

"Hi," I said.

"Hi," he replied.

We had already greeted each other, but the second greeting was more of an acknowledgement of our eye contact.

"Thanks for coming," I said, still looking at him.

"Thanks for inviting me," he said. "It's not every day you meet Ezekiel Tanner."

I had never told him I was related to Uncle E, and I knew he was saying that to let me know he knew.

"Uncle E's not at the game tonight," I said. "But he and Aunt Rhonda want you to stay on their farm. They mentioned it about five times. I hoped you might agree once you figured out who he was."

I glanced at Eric and he grinned at me.

"I knew who he was before I ever bought the horse," Eric said. "Your last name being Tanner and everything, it wasn't that difficult to put the pieces together."

"So much for making you change your mind about staying at the house," I said with a playfully hopeless shrug. I waved at the ladies at the admission table since we had already paid, and Eric and I began making our way past the concessions toward the gym doors. "Aunt Rhonda told me to mention it again just in case. They've got a lot of room. There's an empty apartment next to Jude's."

"I might reconsider if you're staying close by."

Chapter 9

Eric

Olivia wrapped her arms around Eric right when he arrived, and the long day of waiting and traveling was instantly worth it. She was wonderful. The last time he had seen her, her hair was up in a ponytail, and now she was dressed up with her hair mostly down over her shoulders. She had on nice clothes and a little makeup. She still looked natural and innocent, but he could tell she dressed up to see him. She was comfortable in her own skin no matter what, and that was one of the things that attracted him the most.

She met Eric outside, and he followed her into the gymnasium. It was loud, packed, and chaotic. The screeching of sneakers along with crowd noises and cheerleaders chanting all hit him like a wall of noise when they opened the door. He followed close behind Olivia, taking in as much of this over-stimulating situation as he could.

Her family was situated at the top of the bleachers, occupying the space of about three rows. There were a lot of them, and Eric, one-by-one, met them all. He knew Olivia had a big family, but he hadn't quite expected to encounter what must have been twenty of them at the basketball game.

Ezekiel had a scheduled appearance at a conference, so he and Rhonda weren't there, but it seemed like everyone else was. Eric met Olivia's brother, cousins, aunts, uncles and friends, and one thing he noticed as a common thread the whole time was that no one called her Olivia. She had warned him of that, but it still felt odd hearing them call her nothing but Livi. He liked both names on her.

To an extent, Eric knew what to expect. He knew she had a large family and that Ezekiel Tanner was her uncle. He also knew they were going to a high school basketball game that evening and that her cousin, Tanner, was a really good player.

She had downplayed everything, though. She downplayed how cool her family was, how much they loved her, and how fun the whole atmosphere would be. He did not anticipate walking into such a welcoming, fun family situation. They made bets with each other, told stories, laughed, and cut up, and this was all in the first two hours.

It seemed like only seconds passed, and the next thing Eric knew, the game was over and they were headed toward the parking lot.

Tanner's team won the game. They were on a streak and would likely win state. On top of that, Tanner personally had an excellent game. At six-feet-tall, he was not the tallest guy on the team, but he was quick and scrappy, and he was, hands down, the stand-out—the star player.

They had a blast watching him, and they all headed out of the gym in great moods. Eric hadn't touched Olivia at all since the hug when he first got there, but as they walked out of the gym, he felt a gentle pinch to the back of his arm. He turned to look at Olivia who was walking next to him.

"I rode here with Jude," she said. "But if you decide to stay in Uncle E's apartment, I could just ride back with you. I know enough about Lexington to tell you how to get from—"

"I'll stay," he said. "If you're sure I won't be putting anyone out."

"Oh, no, it's an apartment. An empty apartment. My aunt wanted to make sure you knew that. It's like a hotel. There's a microwave and a washer and dryer." Olivia paused so that she could acknowledge the guy who had just walked-up from behind her and tapped on her shoulder.

"How long are you staying?" he asked.

"Till Saturday," she said.

"Okay, maybe I'll see you again before that."

It was a guy who had been introduced to Eric as a friend of the family.

"Yes sir," Olivia said. "I'll be at one more of Tanner's games."

"Oh, yeah, they've got another one Friday, huh?"

"Yes sir."

"Okay, we'll see you again, then. It was nice meeting you," he added, looking at Eric who smiled and returned the sentiment.

She looked at Eric again once that guy walked off. "I'll ride with you if you're staying at the house."

"Okay, I will," he said.

It took a few minutes for them to say goodbye to the family. Olivia admitted that she was only a little sure about how to get back, and right when Eric was saying that they would just search the address, Jude announced that they should just follow him. They discussed stopping for something to eat on the way home, but they had all eaten a hamburger at the game, and none of them felt hungry.

The next thing Eric knew, he was following Jude's pick-up truck down the highway with Olivia sitting in his passenger's seat.

"I love this car. Truck. What do you call this?"

"I like it too," Eric said. "And I don't think it minds being called whatever."

"I know it's an SUV, but I think if I had to choose between calling it a car or a truck, I'd call it a truck. I think it's more truck-y."

Eric nodded, wearing an amused grin.

"What do you call yours at home?" she asked, knowing he drove some variation of a 'Rover' in Philadelphia.

"I don't really know what I think of it," he said. He glanced over his shoulder. "Probably a truck if I had to choose between those two. It's a little bit bigger than this one."

"Oh, that's a truck, then," she said, sounding convinced. He laughed and glanced at her but then focused on the road again. He could feel her looking at him from her seat and he wanted to do something about it—to reach out and touch her.

"Did I hear your brother say that the apartment I'm staying in is right next door to his?" he asked.

"It is," I said. "And they're part of the stables," I said. "So, I hope you're not allergic to horses.

"Your brother already asked me that, and I'm not, but you're underselling it again. You say I'm staying *in the stables*, and it sounds like the manger scene, but I bet it's more like the Ritz-Carlton."

She laughed. "It's not like that," she said. "But, you're right, it's not the manger scene, either."

She paused and then said. "Maybe it is like the Ritz, now that I think about it. I don't know, actually. I've never been to the Ritz. The apartments are really nice, though. They don't smell like horses or anything. And you'll have everything you need. Sometimes I regret not spending a year or two working on Uncle E's farm before jumping into a corporate job." She let out a self-deprecating laugh. "Not that I have anything to complain about," she added. "My really tough corporate job now officially includes doodling on paper cups."

She had already thanked him enough for setting her up with that new position. She knew she didn't have to say it again.

"Lexington seems like a pretty place," he said, changing the subject. "At least in pictures. I couldn't really see anything. It was dark when I got here."

"It's crazy about your flight."

"I know. The weather didn't even seem that bad."

"Was the airport packed?"

"It was, but I didn't have to deal with it. They called me thirty minutes before we were ready for take-off."

"Do airlines do that?"

"It was a plane my dad chartered, but we still have to go by weather advisories. I got out sooner than a lot of other people at the airport, though, everybody's trips were pushed back."

Eric had been talking to Olivia every day for a couple of weeks. They had talked about his trip and he had plenty of opportunity to mention the private plane, but he didn't. Olivia was content to never talk about money. She seemed to purposely avoid the subject, and Eric didn't mind it that way.

They had gotten to know each other. He knew that she was aware of the fact that he came from a wealthy family. She knew what kind of car he drove and that he had an apartment in the city and a second home in the country. Olivia knew those basic things just from asking other questions about how he spent his time. She didn't know the extent of his fortune, though, and she didn't seem to care. Eric liked that about her. She didn't mention his money and she also didn't mention the fact that her uncle was Ezekiel Tanner. He had found that out on his own.

Ezekiel Tanner was kind of a big deal in his household. It was crazy to Eric that Olivia's dad was the man's brother. It was a small world. Eric's father and grandfather were huge Pistons fans back in the day, and Eric's dad met Ezekiel a few times during his prime in the NBA. It was something Eric hadn't told Olivia but would likely mention to Ezekiel once they met.

Growing up rich had its perks. Eric had met his fair share of actors, musicians, and athletes. It would be cool to hang out with Ezekiel Tanner, but that wasn't what was driving him. It was Olivia he had been waiting to see. She was the one who had been on his mind.

Her appearance was a little more polished this evening than it had been in the coffee shop. She had traded her friendship bracelets for subtle gold jewelry, and her hair and makeup were more thoughtful. She still had a youthful innocence about her that made her seem delicate to him. He felt an undeniable urge to be with her—to guard her.

"He's taking you the front way so you can go by the big house," Olivia said once they pulled onto the private road that led into the farm. "That's Uncle E's house," she said, pointing into the distance. The road was lined on both sides with white wooden horse fences. It was beautiful, even in the dark.

"So, there's another entrance that will take you straight to the stables?" Eric asked, following Jude.

"Basically," she said. "We could have kept going down that road and turned left later on. This way's a little longer, but it takes you by the house."

Olivia's phone had begun ringing while she was talking, and she picked it up and put it to her ear once she finished her statement.

"Hey, what's up?" she asked.

She paused, and Eric couldn't hear what was being said on the other end.

"I thought I'd go with you guys. Why?"

A pause.

"Oh, no, I mean, I just assumed I would go with you since Eric's going to meet Mister Everything."

She paused.

"It's okay. I can just walk back later. Or you can take me."

Another pause.

"I'm sure. Okay, bye."

Olivia turned off her phone and set it in her lap. Eric glanced at her, and she smiled and pointed toward the beautiful home they were passing on their left.

"I'm staying in the big house," she explained. "My clothes and everything are there. Jude was asking if I wanted to be dropped off right now."

"How far is it?" Eric asked as they drove slowly through the property.

"It's pretty far," she said. "It's walkable, but they drive or use golf carts most of the time. He was wondering about me getting back."

"Oh, I'm not worried about that," Eric said. "I'll drive you back whenever."

He glanced at her from over the console, and she grinned at him. She was adorable. Her teeth. He wouldn't call them jagged, but they were not lined-up quite like everyone else's. The canines were protruding a little and set slightly higher, giving her whole smile a different, interesting, beautiful appearance. It was one of the things about her that seemed youthful to him—unrefined. He loved the way she looked.

He was happy he had gotten to know her over the phone, but he wished he had a little more practice being around her. As of now, he was still distracted by her beauty. He was glad he had to concentrate on the road because if he had to look at her any longer, he would have reached out and taken her hand.

"I can't believe Jude went that way because he wanted to drop me off," she said. She was shaking her head, Eric could see the motion out of his periphery. "He should have known I would want to see you meet Mister Everything."

"Do I get to meet him tonight?" Eric said.

"Yeah," she said. "Your apartments are right there connected the stables."

"I guess I didn't know if he would be in that same set of stables or not. I wasn't prepared to meet him tonight. I feel like I should bring him a gift or something."

Olivia laughed and the sound of it tugged at his chest.

"Who, Mister Everything?" she asked. "You want to get him a gift?"

"Yeah. What do you buy a racehorse? Does your brother need some nice tack or something for him?"

"How do you know it's called tack?" she asked.

"I don't remember where I learned that. I heard it a long time ago."

"I think my uncle is letting Jude use his stuff," she said.

"He might need some of his own," Eric said. "I'll talk to Jude about it."

Chapter 10

Eric

Eric parked next to Jude once they made it to the stables. The structure in front of him was Spanish inspired and definitely closer to the Ritz than an old, country farm. Eric barely had time to take in his surroundings before Olivia opened her door and began climbing out of the vehicle. He wanted to walk around and open the door for her, but she was too quick.

He had dated a number of women over the years and they had always just gotten into and out of cars by themselves. He had never even given it a second thought. Eric experienced an odd sensation of regret as he stared at Olivia, standing there with the passenger's door open. She was perfectly capable of opening her own car door, and yet he wanted to do it for her—he wanted to take care of her.

"Can I help you with your luggage?" she said, snapping him out of his thoughts.

"No, no, no. I'll get it. I just have one bag." He got out of the driver's side and met Olivia at the back of the vehicle. Jude got out of his truck and joined them over there. They had a conversation with him about the SUV Eric was driving, and Jude ended up sitting in the driver's seat to check it out.

"You guys can come into my place," Jude said as the three of them approached the building. "Your door is number two right there. It's unlocked if you want to set your luggage inside. There's a key on the coffee table in case you want to lock it up on your way out. Nobody will bother your stuff, but the key's there."

"These doors are the apartments?" Eric stopped walking and took in the entrances.

"Yeah, and each unit has a back door that leads into the stables, but you can come meet us at my place when you're done and we'll go in through there."

Jude had some papers for Eric to sign, and he was chomping at the bit for him to do it. Jude knew he could relax and that everything would work out, but it was his first time doing this and he was excited.

Jude and Olivia went into Jude's apartment while Eric went into door number two. It was a nice place with simple, inviting furniture that went with the architecture of the building. Eric set his bag down on the other side of the bed, grabbed the key, and took a glance in the fridge, which was stocked with a few simple snacks and drinks. It was as nice or nicer than any hotel he would have stayed at, and the bonus was the proximity to Olivia. At the thought of her, he turned, closed the fridge, and headed for the door.

Within seconds, he was in Jude's apartment. It was set up exactly like the one he was staying in, except Jude had all his personal stuff lying around. Eric knew he still had some papers to sign, and he was just as excited and anxious to do it as Jude was. He couldn't wait to be a part of all this. This whole atmosphere was already exciting to him.

Jude and Olivia were standing in the kitchen, and Eric went over to join them.

"Is it up to your standards?" Olivia asked.

"I hope so, or I'm unreasonable," Eric replied.

She was teasing him anyway. She had gotten to know him enough that she knew he was easy to please. Eric stared at the papers on the countertop as he approached.

"He's technically ours," Jude said. "But this makes it feel even more official."

"Let's do it," Eric said, glancing around for a pen.

"What are you looking for?" Jude asked, seeing him searching.

"A pen."

"Oh, a pen. Of course, you might need that," Jude said with a nervous laugh. He pointed to the area of cabinet space near Olivia's mid-section. "They're in a drawer right there behind you," he said.

Olivia turned and retrieved a pen from the drawer.

"What'd you think about Tanner's game?" Jude asked.

He asked the question at the exact perfect time because Eric was in the middle of the pen transaction with Olivia, and they paused their efforts while Eric turned to Jude to answer. Their hands were literally touching. It was just their fingertips—where they overlapped as both of them were holding the pen at the same time. Jude's distraction could not have been timed more perfectly, and Eric answered the question, looking at Jude and pretending he was completely unaware of the fingertip touching that was happening with his right hand.

He was not unaware of it.

He was, on the contrary, extremely aware of it.

Heat rose in his chest when he realized that she wasn't moving.

"I loved it," Eric said, with his gaze focused on Jude. "Olivia had told me that he was a good player, but I was blown away. He's amazing."

Jude nodded.

"Is he already committed to UK?" Eric asked, still touching her, hand unmoving.

Jude nodded, but then he glanced at their hands, which made Olivia pull back, leaving the pen in Eric's possession.

"He is," Jude said. "We've got four more years of Wildcat craziness coming."

"Will you stay in Lexington, then? After you graduate?"

Eric knew Jude was the same age as Jordan and would also graduate college that coming May. He knew he had grown up in Philly like Olivia, but Jude never talked about what he would do when he graduated. Olivia glanced at Jude like she was curious as well.

"I really don't know yet," Jude said. "I was dating this girl down here, and I was thinking about staying with her, but we broke up about a month ago. I guess I'll have to see what happens with this horse and then figure out what I'm thinking after that, you know, with a job and everything. I'll be working with him for another year or two, at least."

"Well, I'm excited to see what happens with him." Eric made the statement, pen in hand, as he stared at the paperwork, searching for the place to sign.

Jude showed him where he needed the signatures and then offered them something to drink. They only hung out in the apartment for a minute or two before deciding to go meet the horse.

Mister Everything was all he was cracked up to be. Olivia had met him before, and she was excited to make the introduction to Eric. She was adorable. She was trying not to make it obvious, but Eric could tell she was excited by the way she wiggled and jiggled in these tiny movements that she thought he didn't notice. She smiled a lot, too, and he tried his best not to get lost staring at her mouth, but it was difficult. He imagined what it would be like to kiss her. He had never in his adult life been interested in a woman and gotten to know her to this extent without kissing her.

Eric could tell Olivia liked him, but she did not throw herself at him. They were friends who had long discussions about things that weren't relationships or relational intentions. He wasn't used to women being like that with him. Most of them would have wanted him to define things by now.

Olivia was unlike other women, plain and simple. It had been a long time since he had heart-fluttering feelings, but she did that to him. It was everything about her. He watched how she spoke and how she moved and the way she reacted to things. He knew her voice well, but it was mesmerizing getting the visual to go with it. She was uninhibited, sweet, funny, beautiful.

It was difficult for Eric to pay attention to anything with Olivia around, but it was plain to see that Mister Everything was a gorgeous horse—a fine specimen. He was a stunning creature and Jude explained that he was only about half his eventual weight and would only get better looking as he grew.

Jude and Olivia were both happy and proud, and Eric had more fun watching them make the introduction than looking at the horse.

Seeing as how Mister Everything was a yearling and could easily get stirred, they only stayed a few minutes in his stall. They moved to the next stall to visit a bay mare named Destiny. She was extremely docile, and thus was Olivia's favorite horse on the farm.

Eric asked questions about training, racing, and jockeys, and Jude took pleasure in answering them. All three of them stood in Destiny's stall, talking to each other and visiting with the horse. Jude was on the horse's right side, and Eric was on her left along with Olivia who had been stroking Destiny's neck the whole time they talked.

Eric would reach up periodically and do the same thing, but Olivia never stopped touching the horse. She didn't take her hand from Destiny's short, soft, velvety fur. Her uncle's house was the only time Olivia was ever around horses, and she loved to interact with them as much as she could while she was there. She didn't go into the stalls alone, but as long as Jude or one of the other guys was with her, she was fearless.

Slowly, expertly, she stroked Destiny's neck while Jude and Eric talked. Eric was standing closer to the horse than Olivia was, and he reached up and placed his hand on Destiny's neck. He was saying something to Jude and pretending that he didn't know what he was doing, but he very purposefully put his hand in Olivia's line of trajectory.

He asked Jude a question about stud fees and held still, resting his hand on Destiny, waiting to see if Olivia would touch him. His heart nearly jumped out of his chest when he felt it. He wasn't looking at her or at their hands. His gaze was trained on Jude, but his attention was one hundred percent devoted to the place where her hand came to rest touching his.

It was his pinky, and he could not think of nor focus on anything else.

Olivia's hand moved ever so slowly across Destiny's neck, brushing gently against Eric's pinky. She had been stroking the horse the whole time, but she eventually came to a stop when she came in contact with his hand. Both of their palms were facing down, touching the horse. The only place Olivia touched him was the side of his fingers, and even still, Eric felt out of his head with attraction, desire, love.

Jude was talking, but he sounded like the teacher from Peanuts because all Eric could think of or feel was emanating from his pinky finger. The center of his universe, in that moment, was his pinky. She was touching him. Not moving. She was letting her finger rest next to his. It was fully intentional.

Jude could see their faces but not their hands. He had no idea what was going on—that they were touching. Olivia was brave for leaving her hand there, and it pleased Eric way more than it should have. Eric could not stop himself from glancing at her. He turned and looked her way, staring instantly into her dark eyes.

She held his gaze for an awestruck heartbeat or two, but quickly glanced at her brother with a casual smile.

"But it could be hundreds-of-thousands, right?" Olivia asked Jude, though Eric had no idea what the context was.

Her hand was still touching his.

Jude still had no idea.

Eric was dazed.

He couldn't believe something as innocent as a casual hand-touching could have his chest feeling like it might explode. He had to stop staring at her before he did something crazy like kiss her right there in front of Jude and Destiny. He was on the verge of doing it. He felt like he had to claim her in some way. He had grown close to this girl over the phone, he was invested emotionally. And seeing her, being with her, touching her… it was just too much.

"That's a best-case-scenario," Jude said, referring to Olivia's statement. "That's after a good racing career, and siring some winners. It won't happen overnight."

Eric smiled. "Nothing worth it ever does."

Chapter 11

Eric

He had been getting close to this girl, falling for her, for more than two whole weeks. But who was counting? Either way, it was difficult for Eric to pretend that he and Olivia were just casual acquaintances or business associates. Olivia didn't seem like a casual acquaintance to him at all. She felt like family to him. And now, there she was, touching his hand and giving him all sorts of feelings.

He was alive with anticipation. Her hand rested against the side of his for long enough that it could not be mistaken as an accident. He glanced at her, but not for longer than normal. He was desperate to give his attention to her, to check her out, but couldn't let himself be so obvious.

They continued talking to Jude, and after what must have been a minute or two, she continued moving. Her hand ran from his pinky down the side of his hand as she continued petting Destiny. Eric cleared his throat when she finally moved, and it caused her to smile.

They made discreet hand contact like this for the span of half an hour while hanging out with Destiny and carrying on a conversation with Jude. Olivia asked her brother questions that required detailed answers—questions she didn't necessarily care about the answers to.

Jude eventually moved and came around to their side of the horse, putting an end to their game. They stopped to meet a few of the other horses during the tour of the stables and each time, their hands accidentally touched. It was fun trying to find ways to touch each other without her brother seeing them. Olivia certainly wasn't shying away from Eric's efforts. If anything, she was encouraging it to happen.

The tour of the stables took over an hour, and they naturally made their way toward the apartments afterward.

"I should go ahead and get you back to the big house," Jude said, obviously talking to Olivia.

"I could take her over there," Eric said.

"Oh, no, thank you, but I have to go in and talk to Uncle E, anyway. I texted him earlier and told him I was gonna drop that paperwork by. He's waiting for me."

Olivia was annoyed with her brother. There was no paperwork that needed to be taken care of at this hour. Uncle E wasn't waiting for the paperwork, it was Jude who was overly-zealous about getting it to him, and Olivia knew it. She didn't say anything, though. Eric had been traveling and meeting new people, and she was sure he was tired anyway.

But Eric wasn't tired.

He could have stayed up all night, talking to her, looking at her.

Neither of them said anything to stop Jude's plan, and before long, both of them were gone and Eric was alone in his apartment.

He felt lonely for her, and he reminded himself that he would have been in the same situation if he had gone to his hotel.

He had pursued things in business and in life but he never felt the urge to pursue a woman like this.

What he found next made it even worse.

Eric found an envelope in the bathroom of the apartment where he was staying. His name was on it, and he saw it the second he turned on the light. Eric wore an easy smile as he pulled the card from the envelope. It was one of Olivia's drawings. It was a man standing next to a horse in the winner's circle. It was stylized, but it was certainly the likeness of him standing next to Mister Everything.

Olivia normally used black pen and mostly outlines with light shading in her drawings, but this one had color. The whole thing almost had the look of a cast iron toy. It looked a little like it had been done in pastels, but it hadn't smeared when he pulled it out of the envelope. He thought it might be watercolor.

Eric turned it, inspecting it from different angles. It pleased him to be made into a drawing. He loved that Olivia was talented in this way. He felt like he and that horse had already won just from looking at that drawing of them in the winner's circle. Even if nothing came of the horse, this memento would always be special to him. It was on heavy cardstock and beautifully executed, and he knew he would have it framed.

He was so taken by the outside of the card that he forgot it was a card at all. He opened it and stared at the handwriting inside. It was a beautiful combination of cursive and print, and it was meticulously spaced and even. There were no lines, and he stared at the perfect rows of writing, wondering how she had made it so perfect. He scanned to the bottom of the note and saw her signature with the big letter O. His gaze went back to the top where he began reading.

Eric,

Congratulations on your new horse! And thank you, from the bottom of my heart, for trusting and helping my brother. I don't think you'll be disappointed. I am excited to see what adventure awaits you guys and Mister Everything. I think it's going to be great!

Olivia

The entire card was beautiful to look at. Eric stared at the outside again before opening it and reading it a second time. *When had she made this? When had she put it into the apartment?* She had to have done it earlier, before he ever decided to stay there. He had hardly taken his eyes off of her since they came together earlier that night. He knew she hadn't put the note in his room since they got home from the game. He racked his brain, and came to the conclusion that she had put it in the room when he still had plans to get a hotel. It intrigued him that she would just let him find it and not mention it at all. She had obviously spent a lot of time on the little work of art and most people would have said something about it—told him that it was waiting in his room and made sure he knew to look for it.

He was intrigued by Olivia, taken with her.

They had already said goodnight and made plans to get together in the morning for breakfast, but he couldn't help himself. He sent her a text.

Eric:
I love this card. Thank you. And I had fun tonight. Thanks for that too.

He sent it to her, and he kept his phone handy because he thought he might hear back quickly.

But that wasn't the case. He kept an eye on his phone for the next half hour or so, but Olivia didn't text him back. There was nothing to do but go on with his evening. He returned some texts and emails before showering and changing, and then he turned on the television.

It was 11pm when he heard back from her. His phone was sitting beside him on the bed when it dinged. The Tanners had a couple of streaming services hooked to his television and he chose a cooking show to space out on before he fell asleep. He had just about given up on hearing back from Olivia when her return text came through.

Olivia:

I am so sorry I'm just seeing this. I was visiting with Aunt Rhonda and my phone was in my purse. I'm happy you liked the card and that you had fun. I did too. Congratulations on the horse!

Eric wasn't even finished reading it when the second text came in.

He read the first and then went down to the second which said:

Olivia:

Oh, no. Sorry about how late it is. I sent before I even looked at the time. Rest well.

He stared at the phone with an absentminded smile as he typed out the reply.

Eric:

How did you get that card into the apartment?

Olivia:

I left it in there this afternoon.

Eric:
I almost went to a hotel.

Olivia:
I would have given it to you tomorrow.

Eric:
It's a masterpiece. It's sitting on my bedside table. I'll frame it when I get home.

Olivia took a little longer to reply—maybe a minute or so.

Olivia:
It makes me happy that you like it. I'm really glad you're here.

Eric:
Me too. It took too long to see you.

It was a little bold, but Eric felt brave or impatient, or perhaps both.

Olivia:
I agree. It was a relief seeing you today.

Eric gripped the phone tightly when he read her words. He experienced urges at the thought of her being relieved. He rested his head on the back of the headboard with a sigh, staring at the ceiling for a few seconds while he gathered his thoughts. He thought of a few responses, but nothing shy of *please come back over here* seemed right.

Eric spent a minute trying to think of something to say. He wanted to see Olivia again that night, but he didn't know if it was okay to come out and ask her if he could. While he was working up the nerve, Olivia assumed she had said too much and sent a text trying to explain.

Olivia:
It just seems like we've been talking forever on the phone. It was crazy putting a face to your voice.

Eric: I was relieved, too. I don't know why we didn't meet up in Philly.

Olivia:
I'm better here, anyway. (Smiley face.) It's better that we connect here. This life here is better than my Philly life.

Eric's fear when he read her text was that she wouldn't want to see him once they got home. This was obviously unacceptable.

Eric:
What's that mean?

Olivia:

I don't know. Just that my Kentucky family is fun. I'm glad you're getting to see this side of my life.

Eric wanted to know that he'd be able to see her once they went back to Philadelphia. He wanted to make her promise that.

Eric:
What about the other side of your life? Will you be glad for me to see that?

Olivia:
Not really.

Eric:
Why not?

Olivia: I'm not un-glad about it, but I'm cooler in KY. You and I can just hook up here twice a year.

Eric:
Can I talk to you?

Olivia:
On the phone?

Eric:
No.

Olivia:

Do you want to come over here?

Eric:

Yes.

Olivia:

Meet me at the front entrance of my uncle's in ten minutes.

Eric replied with a simple, "Yes," and instantly sprang off the bed.

Chapter 12

Olivia

I was waiting at the front door when I saw Eric's Rover pull into the circle driveway. It was cold out, and all I had on was a pair of thermal pajamas, so I stayed inside to wait for him.

I stood by the door and watched him approach. I knew the code to their home alarm, so I made sure it was switched off before unlocking the door.

Eric smiled when he saw the door open. He was in street clothes—jeans and boots with a jacket— mostly the same clothes he had on at the game. He had taken a shower, though. I could tell because he had a different t-shirt on and his hair was laying differently.

"I thought you said you'd rather be called Olivia," was the first thing he said to me as he came up the steps toward the door.

"I would rather be called that. Why?"

I spoke at a normal volume. My aunt and uncle had gone to bed, but their house was gigantic, and there was no way they could hear us. There were enough lights on in the house to see where you were going, but it was much darker now than it was when everybody was awake. Eric followed me inside, and I watched as he looked around.

"Nice," he said. I stared at the side of his face—at the lines and curves, at the subtle indention of his cheek and the dusting of short facial hair that grew there. It was difficult to do anything but stare at him. My body experienced sensations that made a nervous smile cross my face.

"You can hang your jacket right in here," I said, opening the nearby coat closet.

Eric stepped inside like he knew just what to do. He expertly shed his jacket and shoes and stashed them out of the way.

We walked out of the closet. I headed for the den where we would find a huge living area with comfortable couches and chairs. "Why'd you say that about my name?" I asked.

"Because you were saying your life was better down here."

"It is. Kind of."

"But everybody here calls you Livi."

I laughed at his logic. "My life being better down here doesn't have anything to do with my name," I said.

"What's it have to do with?" he asked.

"It's not that my life is better, necessarily. It's just different." I gestured around us, to the sprawling mansion with marble floors. "This doesn't exist in my normal life. My dad is Uncle E's brother, but it doesn't translate to anything material. My dad doesn't live like this. He's got an apartment. He works at a home improvement store."

We were silent for a few seconds as we walked, and I glanced at Eric when we approached the den.

"Is that supposed to mean I won't be able to see you in Philadelphia? That's what I don't understand."

I shook my head, but I also shrugged a little. "I'm happy with the things I've accomplished in my life so far. I love my mom and dad and everything, but they're different than this. My life's not this cool in Philly. I'm not saying it's bad there, it's just different. All the basketball games and autographs and matching pajamas, all of that disappears in Philadelphia."

"Your aunt and uncle wear matching pajamas?" he asked.

We came around the front of the couch, and I laughed as we sat down. I plopped down, into the corner of the couch with a sigh. This sectional was deep and wide with fluffy pillows—the epitome of comfort. Eric sat close to me on the cushion next to mine. I stared at him. I wasn't normally the type to think I wasn't good enough for someone just because of how much money they had, but I had to be honest this time. Things were different in Kentucky than they were in Philadelphia.

"I wasn't talking about my aunt and uncle having matching pajamas," I said. "I meant me. I meant these. Aunt Rhonda had them waiting on the bed for me when I arrived. I think they're made of some kind of bamboo. Even the clothes I had on tonight at the game were Stella's."

I stopped talking and sat there, waiting to see how Eric would respond. I was a little shy saying those things, so my eyes had been roaming. I had been glancing all around, at the couch and at his knees and feet and hands.

"This is the fairy tale section of my life," I added when the thought crossed my mind.

"Come here," he said.

My gaze snapped up to meet his. His eyes sparkled mischievously even though he wasn't quite smiling.

"I am here," I said.

The hint of a smile touched Eric's lips, and I had to hold myself back from throwing myself into his arms. He seemed to be asking for that.

"Come all the way here," he said nudging his chin at me.

The couch was soft, and I scooted somewhat awkwardly toward him. My leg was cocked-up onto the couch, and I landed with my knee overlapping his leg a little bit.

"Is that what you mean?" I asked, seeming calm even though my heart was beating a mile a minute thanks to all the leg touching.

"Not quite, but it's better than nothing."

"I'm basically on your lap," I said, wearing a deadpan expression that made his face break into a wide smile.

"Yeah, no you're not. That's the problem."

"I just told you this isn't my real life," I said. "Shouldn't we take a second to figure out how you feel about that?"

"I don't need a second," he said. "I know immediately that I don't feel anything about it. I'm not concerned with what you buy, or wear, or what kind of house your dad lives in. I really hope you weren't saying that because you think I wouldn't want to see you in Philadelphia for reasons like that."

"I mean, when you put it like that."

He smiled. "There's no other way to put it." He put his hand on my knee. It was big and warm—I could feel it's warmth the instant he set it on my leg. "I don't care what pajamas you're wearing, Olivia, if they match or not, or what house you're sitting in. You could be in a hut in a hammock." He paused and tilted his head. "I'd like to see you like that, actually."

I smiled. "I'm normally not self-conscious about my life. It's just that you're you, and well, now you have this to compare it to. I just wanted to warn you that my dad and his brother are not alike."

"I've been warned, then. I'll consider myself warned."

"And you still want to…" I trailed off, hoping he would finish that sentence.

"Kiss your mouth? Yes."

He was so casual and unrepentant with his statement that I let out a little laugh.

"Oh, wow," I said, giggling.

"What? I thought I was going to get to."

"And then what?" I asked. I didn't mean to ask for some kind of commitment, but that was how it sounded, so maybe that was what I wanted. "I mean like tomorrow. With my brother and just tomorrow in general. In the daylight. Is it going to be awkward between us? Because I don't want things to be—"

I could not finish the remainder of that sentence. In one quick but gentle motion, Eric leaned toward me. He took a hold of the front of my pajamas and pulled me toward him. I easily let it happen, giving way to the momentum that carried me. I toppled toward him, and he was there to catch me. Our mouths connected like there was a gentle gravitational pull. Our contact was gentle but swift and intentional. He let his lips soften against mine and kept them that way for two or three seconds before pulling back to look at me.

He tilted his head a little, looking thoughtful.

"I'd like to know what to say to make you understand that we don't need to talk about your pajamas or your father's money ever again."

I stared into his gorgeous green eyes. "Because you don't care about any of that?" I asked, blinking at him and feeling shy and hopeful.

He shook his head almost imperceptibly. "I don't care about it," he assured me.

"I just don't want things to be awkward between us," I said, fishing for him to kiss me again like he did the last time I said it.

"Why would you think things would be awkward?" he asked.

"I don't," I said. "I was just trying to say that again since last time something good happened."

I could see that he understood what I was saying. He smiled and shook his head at me. We stared at each other for several seconds before he pulled me closer.

Eric did all the work. He resituated with me leaning halfway on his lap and he held me captive in his arms. He pulled me close, staring down at me, our bodies touching, his arms around me. His t-shirt was thin and I could feel the ridges of muscles in his arms and core. He smelled nice, and that combined with the feel of his warm body around mine was a delight to the senses. My face was right next to his, and I stared at him feeling thankful for and relieved by our proximity.

I was exactly where I wanted to be. It was overwhelming being there. I had been aching for him, and the release of finally being next to him left me with an urgent feeling. I wanted our bodies to meld together. If it was humanly possible in that moment I might have crawled inside him. I had felt close to Eric many times over the phone, but nothing compared to being in his arms.

He kissed me. He did it slowly at first and then it built into something more urgent, fluid. I turned in his arms, taking his face in my palms, touching his cheeks gently. We kissed for several blood-racing moments before he pulled back. Tenderly, he leaned in and kissed me twice and then a third time before pulling back again.

"What were you saying about things being awkward?" he asked.

"I didn't want—"

He kissed me suddenly. He moved swiftly, stealing a quick but light kiss on my mouth.

"Things to get—"

He did it again.

Another kiss.

Two that time.

"Weird between—"

Kiss.

"During the day with my brother and—"

Kiss. Once, twice, three, four, five, six... ten times before pulling back to stare at me.

"What was I even saying?" I asked dazedly.

Eric smiled and I saw the flash of white teeth.

"This is definitely the fairytale section of my life," I said. I meant to think it, but I was almost positive I said it out loud.

"Do you mean what we're doing right here?" Eric asked.

Yep. I had said it out loud.

I nodded.

"This isn't a fairytale," he said.

"This is at least as good as a fairytale," I said, glancing around at my current situation.

"It's as good as a fairytale, but you better not think it's not real," he said. "I hope you don't think it's temporary."

I squinted playfully at him. "I don't think it's temporary, I just, you know, it's new. We're feeling each other out."

"Oh, so, you're just feeling me out?" he said with a casual, confident grin. His arms were still around me.

"What should I call this if it's not a fairytale?"

"Life," he said.

I smiled. "It's funny how life works. God and everything."

"I was just thinking about God," he said.

"Really?"

"Yeah. I mean, it's hard not to. There were Bible verses in about four different places in that apartment. There's at least two in this room. Everywhere I look there's a Bible verse."

I laughed, knowing he was right.

"I think God had to do with you coming here—doing this with my brother," I said. "My aunt prayed about my brother getting a miracle with an investor, and I feel like me getting to meet you is sort of a side effect to my brother's miracle."

"Me meeting you is definitely not the smaller of those two miracles," he said. "I wouldn't call it the side effect. I think we were God's main intention here. If anything, the horse is a side-miracle to us."

I smiled. "You think so?"

He smirked at my hopefulness. "I know so," he said. "You're the best part of being here, Olivia. The horse is fun and everything, and your family's cool, but you're my goal, you're what I'm after, you know that, right?"

I didn't know how to answer or if I should. I felt speechless. How had I ended up here? How had two people like us from Philadelphia ended up on my uncle's couch in Kentucky?

"Do you like me back, Olivia?" Eric asked, point blank, utterly confident.

"Yes," I said, feeling vulnerable with our faces only a foot or so apart. "I like you very much."

His chest rose and fell with a measured breath. I watched as his eyes closed slowly. "Can you say that again?" he asked, smiling a little like he was taking it all in.

Chapter 13

I stretched upward, leaning toward Eric. "I like you very much," I repeated, my mouth right next to his ear. His eyes were closed, as far as I knew. His hands were wrapped around me—one on my side and one on my knee, and I felt his grip tighten when I whispered in his ear.

"Just once more," he said.

He was completely still, waiting for me to speak. I kept my mouth right next to his ear. "I like you so much, Eric."

I felt muscles in his whole body slowly grow tense as I spoke, and it pleased me so much that I continued. "I like that you're competitive and smart. You have good ideas and you work hard, and you have good taste."

He did. I had come to admire his taste. He didn't just like things because they were expensive either, he really did have thoughtful, exquisite taste. We talked about things we liked and why we liked them and I had come to admire his way of thinking. Everything was a little easier to process when our relationship was based on talking on the telephone, though. Now that we were in each other's physical company, I wanted him even more.

Things that didn't bother me before, when our relationship was strictly on the phone, came to mind now that I was sitting in his arms. For instance, he had a date coming up to go to a major award show with another woman, and before this moment, it didn't bother me at all.

Elle Wallace was her name.

She was the daughter of Jimmy Wallace, who, as you probably already know is the lead singer of the Kooks.

The Wallace family was originally from Philadelphia. Eric and Elle had met when they were teenagers and had remained friends ever since. He had been to award shows with her before. Usually, she went with whoever she was dating, but Eric had stepped-in a few times over the years when she didn't have another date. He told me about his upcoming date with Elle only a few days into our friendship, and I assured him that I thought it was the coolest thing in the world that he got to go to the Grammys. I reacted like I didn't have any personal feelings about it at all.

But now that I was sitting on his lap with his arms wrapped around me, I had a whole host of personal feelings. I thought of Eric walking the red carpet in a couple of weeks with Elle and Jimmy, and I felt a pang of jealousy.

"Do you like me back?" I whispered into his ear in a moment of doubt.

Eric's grasp had tightened when I whispered into his ear. He pulled back to look at me. "I like you so much," he said. "It-it actually hurts a little." He gestured to his own chest.

I wanted to ask him right then and there not to go to the Grammys with Jimmy Wallace's daughter, but since that would come out of nowhere, I didn't say it.

"Come here," he said, giving me a quick, light squeeze.

"I'm here," I said glancing at the fact that I was leaning against him, partially on his lap. "I'm about as here as I can get."

"I meant kiss me."

"Oh, is that what you meant?" I asked sounding confident. "Because you could've just said so."

"Kiss me, Olivia." He said the words in a neutral, no-nonsense tone that had my heart racing. It was gentle enough, but he was sure of himself. "Please," he added as if remembering his manners.

I was aching to do it, but I felt shy. I smiled and leaned upward an inch or two, aiming for his mouth but not getting there. I went back to where I was after the futile attempt at a kiss, and he scowled playfully at me.

I grinned.

He was irresistible.

He was all put together but not in an untouchable way—he was down-to-earth and approachable for someone who could easily come across as unobtainable.

"What was that?" he asked, talking about my fruitless motion. "That was terrible. You completely missed."

"I'm shy."

"You're not shy," he said. "We've been sitting here kissing already, and you weren't shy then."

"That's because you were in charge." I said.

He let out a little amused laugh as he pulled back, readjusting as he leaned back on the couch. He was farther from me now. His head was about a foot away instead of inches. He acted casual like the distance was just a byproduct of him getting comfortable, but I knew what he was doing. Now that I said I was shy, he was playing with me, making me go to him.

"You went way over there," I said.

"I had to get comfortable."

"You need to put your face a little closer," I said.

"I could say the same thing to you," he said.

Suddenly, I turned and collapsed back, letting my upper body fall across his chest, lying across him. My movement was so unexpected that Eric reacted the way I hoped he would and caught me. He leaned in, cradling me across his lap like a baby in his arms. As a result of my momentum he was now leaning forward and his face was only inches from mine again. This time, I felt like I was almost under him.

I reached up and wrapped my hand around the back of his head, pulling him toward me while at the same time, stretching upward to meet him. Our lips touched gently, but then I leaned closer and pulled him toward me, and we connected more deeply. He took over from there, opening his mouth, drawing me in, kissing me with rhythmically gentle passion. I laid across his lap and he leaned over me, kissing me for several long moments.

We didn't talk.

We never stopped.

We never broke contact.

We sat there and kissed each other.

Finally, after what must have been fifteen or fifty-two dizzying minutes, Eric pulled back. He was the best kisser in the entire world, and he was gorgeous. I already felt like I was in love with the man I had been getting to know on the phone, but seeing him, being with him, this put things over the top for me. I had been trying not to get my hopes up, but now I felt like I had to have him. It just wouldn't be okay for me to live my life without him.

We readjusted again and started talking about work—about the coffee shop. He liked to know my honest opinion about how things ran and what I thought he could do to make it smoother or better.

I enjoyed working there, and it was something that was fun for me to talk about with him. We talked about my plans for a series of lucky cups. He was excited about doing something new and unexpected for his customers, and it made me happy to think that he liked one of my ideas and wanted to use it for his whole chain. We sat on that couch talking about the coffee shop for at least an hour. We kissed quite a bit earlier on, but we were not kissing, thank goodness, when my uncle walked into the den.

"Hey Uncle E," I said when I saw him walk into the room. I wasn't sitting across Eric's lap at the moment. But I was close to him—we were obviously close enough to each other that we were being friendly and familiar.

I knew Uncle E didn't care. I was a grown woman, and we weren't doing anything wrong. Still, he regarded us with a serious expression.

"This is Eric," I said.

Uncle E knew we were expecting Eric and that he was staying in the apartment. He knew who Eric was, but he still wore a slightly uncertain expression. Eric got to his feet, but he stayed by the couch not knowing whether he should cross the room shake Uncle E's hand or stay where he was.

"Are you okay?" I asked, resituating on the couch so I could talk to my uncle.

He nodded. "I saw on my phone that the alarm hadn't been set. I thought you had gone to bed, but I wanted to make sure."

"No, I was going to set it… in a minute… once he… heads back."

Eric made a nodding motion at Uncle E. Their house was gigantic, and Uncle E was on the other side of the expansive den, so the two men didn't come together. It was late, and they settled for gesturing at each other from across the distance.

"It's nice to meet you," Eric said. "I'm sorry about the late hour. I'll go ahead and go back so you can set your alarm. I hope we didn't keep you up."

"You didn't," Uncle E said. "I stay up this late all the time. I just thought Livi must've forgotten to set the alarm."

"I didn't," I said, getting to my feet. I stood next to Eric, both of us regarding my larger-than-life uncle. We were grown adults and everything, but with the way Uncle E was looking at us, I thought he might be a little taken aback by the fact that Eric was here so late. That made me even more grateful we had not been kissing.

"I'll set the alarm," I said. "I'm sorry, Uncle E. You can go back to bed."

His serious expression softened a little as he gave me a small nod. "Okay. It's nice to meet you Eric. I appreciate what you're doing for Jude. I'll shake your hand in the morning."

"My pleasure," Eric said ducking his head in another slight bowing motion.

"I guess I'll see you two in the morning." Uncle E said. He gave us a small smile and nod before turning to head to his bedroom.

"Night," I said.

"Night," he returned.

He wasn't upset, but he also wasn't as happy-go-lucky as I had sometimes seen him. Eric and I both told Uncle E goodnight, but that was all we said until he rounded the corner.

We looked at each other once he was out of sight. Both of us had been taken by surprise by his sudden appearance.

"He's fine," I said. "He's just tired."

"There could have been better ways to meet him, I guess, but it's okay. I should be going anyway," Eric said. I knew it was the truth, but it didn't make it easy to say goodbye. I already missed him and we were standing right next to each other. I got a yearning sensation just thinking about it, and it caused me to reach out and touch him. My hand went to his side, just above his waist, and I grabbed a hold of his shirt. He put his hand on my hand, cupping it around mine.

"Thank you," he said.

"For what?" I asked, shifting my weight from foot to foot.

He reached out and touched my waist, holding me steady. "For talking to me about Roxy's. For bringing me here. For everything."

"You're welcome," I said.

He grinned at me. "Walk me to the door."

Eric had a hold of my hand from when I grabbed his shirt, and he didn't let go of me as we started walking toward the door. He stopped once we crossed two rooms and made it there. He put on his jacket and boots.

"I'll say goodbye here," he said before either of us opened the door.

"Goodnight," I said. "Sleep well."

"You too." He pulled me by the hand and used my momentum to draw me into a kiss. I could see and feel what he was doing, so I gave into it, lunging forward to kiss him. It was all so easy and natural.

"I'll see you in a little while," I said. "In the morning."

"Okay, I'll come around nine for breakfast."

I nodded, and with his free hand, Eric reached out for the doorknob. He had to step that way to reach it, and I let him go, smiling even though I didn't want him to leave.

We said goodbye and waved at each other as the door closed, and just like that, he was gone.

I turned and leaned against the door, smiling at the flashes of memories that began to play across my mind.

The basketball game.

The horses.

The accidental hand touching.

Then he comes over.

The couch.

The talking.

The kissing.

Goodness.

His kiss.

I put my hands over my mouth, feeling the urge to giggle or squeal or perform some other ridiculous love-struck behavior.

I found it difficult to fall asleep that night.

I was thinking so much that it took me forever to finally drift off.

Chapter 14

Eric

Eric didn't get to sleep until after 2am that night. This meant he only got four hours of sleep. In spite of his laid-back appearance, he was a shrewd businessman. He was an early riser who always got a lot done during morning hours. It was normal for him to wake up at 6am like he did today, but he didn't usually stay up so late.

Last night was different. He could not fall asleep. He kept staring at the ceiling, thinking about Olivia. He thought about everything she said and remembered specific things she brought up about the coffee shop. Three different times, he sat up to make a note about it.

He remembered her smile and her touch and her kiss, and he could not fall asleep. He turned his alarm off, but his body was so accustomed to waking up at six that he woke up without it. He laid there until 6:30 trying to fall back asleep, but it was useless. His mind continued to race.

Eric resolved to get up and make some notes and take care of some things regarding the coffee shop. He had some other business that also needed his attention. It was probably only an hour's worth of work, so he decided to get up and get it over with.

After that, he would get dressed and walk around the farm for a while until it was time to go to the big house for breakfast.

He had just sat up in the bed and was thinking about coffee being his first objective when he heard a hard pounding on the door. It was the pounding of a heavy fist, and Eric got to his feet instantly. He walked toward the door in a defensive straight-postured stance. The sound had startled him and he felt like there must be some sort of mistake.

The door did not have a peephole, so he went to the nearby window and pulled back the curtain to peer outside. He speculated it was Ezekiel Tanner before he ever saw the giant of a man standing there.

Just when Eric peeked through the crack in the curtain, Ezekiel lifted his hand to knock on the door again. Eric headed for the door right away so that he could avoid the booming sound, but he didn't make it in time. He jolted across the short distance to the door, but he wasn't fast enough. That same heavy pounding sound happened twice before Eric could unlock the door and open it.

The super star basketball player was standing on the other side of the door. Ezekiel had been across a huge room when they met the night before, and he was even larger up close.

"Good morning, Eric."

Cold air rushed in with the open door, and Eric instantly motioned for Ezekiel to come inside.

"Good morning," Eric said. "Would you like to come in?"

"No, thank you. I'm headed to the stables." Ezekiel gestured to his right, toward the main entrance of the stables. "Take your time getting dressed, and you can meet me in there. Will a half hour or so work?"

"Yes," Eric said without skipping a beat. "Just give me ten minutes to put on some clothes and make a cup of coffee."

"I'll make a pot of coffee in the stable kitchen," Ezekiel said.

"Okay, well, five minutes, then."

"Sounds perfect. I'll see you in a minute."

Ezekiel walked away, and Eric went straight to action. He brushed his teeth and ran a comb and a little bit of product through his hair. He put on jeans, an undershirt, a long sleeve thermal, and a jacket. It was warmer in the stables than it was outside, but he wasn't sure what Ezekiel had planned and he wanted to be prepared.

He walked out of the back door of the apartment—the one that led directly into the stables.

He heard Ezekiel's singing coming from a door on the left. It was quite a ways off, but Ezekiel was belting it out loud enough to be heard.

"Country rooooads, take me hoooome to the plaaaace I beloooong, West Virginia, mountain mama, take me hoooome, country rooooads…"

He was humming the tune of the verse when Eric came into the open doorway of the kitchen. It was light in the room—a large, open kitchen and dining area. There was a long table over to one side, but the room was large enough that it still felt airy and open. Ezekiel was on the right, standing in front of the coffee pot, staring at it, singing.

"Country rooooads…" He started into the chorus again, but he saw Eric's movement in the doorway from the corner of his eye, and he stopped singing, looking that way as Eric came into the door.

"Good morning," he said, smiling at Eric. His demeanor was perhaps a little too chipper for six-thirty in the morning. Eric tried not to overthink it. Maybe Ezekiel was just the type to entertain out-of-town guests early in the morning. Maybe he wanted to talk about horses.

"Good morning," Eric responded.

Ezekiel already had two mugs on the counter, and he poured coffee into them as he spoke. "Are you an early riser?" he asked.

"I am," Eric said. "I woke up without the alarm this morning."

"I did too," Ezekiel replied. "I like to make it out onto the farm before sunrise. Being outside during this hour before dawn is my favorite part of the day. I look forward to it."

"I bet it's beautiful on this farm," Eric said.

"It is," Ezekiel said. "You'll see. We'll go over to the covered arena. There's a walking path. It's one of my favorite spots."

"Should I grab gloves and a hat."

"You can. Or we might have an extra set somewhere around here." Ezekiel pushed the mug of black coffee toward Eric who took it gratefully. Neither of them discussed cream or sugar. Both of them just silently began to sip their black coffee. "You can stop at the apartment and get your stuff if you like. It's pretty cold, and we'll be outside."

Eric nodded. "Are we waiting on Jude?"

"No, it's just you and me this morning."

It was obvious the man wanted to talk to Eric about something. Eric didn't know if it was about doing business with Jude or if it was about Olivia, but he would find out soon enough.

"I've met your dad," Ezekiel said, drawing Eric from his thoughts.

They had a ten-minute conversation about Ezekiel's encounter with Eric's father while they drank their coffee, and as soon as Ezekiel took the last sip of his, he put his mug in the sink and announced that they should go.

They stopped to get Eric's cold weather gear and they headed out in Ezekiel's truck. It was still dark out, and they drove across the farm with the headlights on. Ezekiel talked about some of the daily routines on the farm. Once they got closer to their destination, he explained that there was a paved walking path that encompassed the covered arena and three paddocks. Six times around the whole circle made a mile, and Ezekiel liked to walk it in the morning. He enjoyed the view of the sunrise across the hills.

Eric had not planned on walking a mile this morning, but his hiking boots were comfortable, and he knew he would go along with pretty much whatever Ezekiel had planned.

They parked in front of the covered arena and got out of the truck. Ezekiel led the way, expecting Eric to follow, which he did. They set off on the walking path. There was no other action on the farm at the moment, but it was a big place and Eric got the feeling it would be busier around there once the sun came up.

They talked as they walked, Ezekiel asking the questions. They spoke about business investments at first, and then Ezekiel began to ask somewhat more personal questions.

He asked about Eric's family—how many there were, where were they from, what kind of family traditions they had. Still, it all seemed like a normal conversation to have with someone who was visiting your home—someone you were trying to get to know.

They were on their third lap when Ezekiel said, "I'm going to get real with you for a few minutes, if you don't mind, Eric."

And there it was. Eric knew there had to be something behind the early morning wake-up call—some deeper-than-surface-level issue motivating the heavy fist that pounded on his door.

"I don't mind at all," Eric said even though he felt suddenly wary and defensive.

"I noticed you with my niece last night."

"Yes sir," Eric said, keeping things simple and respectful.

"I heard Livi mention you a few times since she's been here. I hear her talking to her brother or my wife."

Eric felt pleasure that she was talking about him when he wasn't there. He had to hold back a smile.

"I probably wouldn't be having this conversation with you, Eric, if I thought my brother would do it. But I don't think he will. I love my brother, and I know he loves Livi, but for reasons we don't need to get into right now, I feel somewhat like I need to represent my niece as her father figure. I'm not trying to put you on the spot or make you uncomfortable, but I think you might be more than just Jude's business partner in Livi's eyes, and I wanted to have a conversation with you about that. Could you just humor me and let that happen since I love her and feel a sense of responsibility?"

He glanced at Eric, who gave a nod and said, "Yes."

"Do you like my niece?" Ezekiel asked.

"Yes, I do," Eric answered thoughtfully.

"I'm glad to hear you say that," Ezekiel said. "You seem like a nice young man. I just kind of wanted to talk to you and feel you out about it. See where you stood, and make sure you knew she had people who cared about her."

"I know she does."

"We know who your father is and that you have financial stability and everything, but there's so much more to life than that, and Rhonda and I care enough about Livi to look out for her. Like I said, if I thought my brother would do it, I wouldn't be having this conversation with you."

"Is this where you tell me that if I hurt your niece in any way you'll hunt me down and string me from a tree?"

Ezekiel laughed. "Kind of," he said. "I mean not really. I know young people are going to have interests that change. I know people date and break up. I'm not asking you to make any promises. I just wanted you to know Livi has people who love her and care about her and are looking out for her. I also wanted to make sure you heard it from me that I attribute my successful life to God, Eric. Everything you see here is a gift. It is not of my own power that I obtained or maintain any of it. I work hard, don't get me wrong, but my marriage, and my work, and my life all fall in line and flourish because God is at the center of it. It all goes back to Him. Life's difficulties would be painful and confusing without Him."

Ezekiel paused and they walked for a few seconds in silence before he spoke again.

"Again, I don't know where you stand with all that, and I'm not trying to put you on the spot. I just wanted to let you know those things. That Livi has people who care about her and want the best for her. My brother cares about his daughter obviously, but we're different people and he might never pull you aside and tell you that. And I love Livi like she's my own."

"I like that you're looking out for her," Eric said. "And Olivia has talked to me about God a lot. We both think God had something to do with us meeting the way we did."

Eric glanced at Ezekiel in time to catch him grinning. This caused Ezekiel to reach out and tussle Eric's hair, which was one of the highest compliments he could have given right then.

Chapter 15

Olivia

The trip to Lexington came and went, and just like that, I was back in Philly—back to my normal life. In the time since we came back, I had seen Eric nearly every day.

We were together non-stop on the trip, and it was too difficult to go back to our lives the way they were before. We truly enjoyed spending time together. We had fun together. We were, no doubt, attracted to each other, but it wasn't all about that.

We seemed to purposely avoid moments of physical temptation. We spent a lot of time together just being goofy, being friends, and talking and getting to know each other. It was obvious that both of us wanted to get to know each other physically, but we intentionally took it slow.

We kissed every time we saw each other, but it was at the end of our encounter and they were always really light. The kiss we shared the first night at Uncle E's was by far the most passionate. Eric and I had pulled back the reigns after that night, and while I couldn't help but feel certain urges, I knew it was for the best.

We had been spending time getting to know each other, which I felt was almost more of a commitment from him than a physical relationship.

I finished my first batch of lucky cups, but they hadn't been distributed yet. They would be introduced in the middle of February. Eric had a sign made for the register area revealing the concept. Janet, my new supervisor, was tasked with designing that sign, and it was surreal having her work on something that announced an idea of mine.

I never told any of my coworkers at Stone Lion that lucky cups were my idea. I figured they might hear it through the grapevine since Roxy's was downstairs. But so far, I didn't think any of them knew.

The last half of January passed in a blur. Between working two jobs, and making time for my friends and family, I had a busy existence before I ever met Eric. But making time to spend with him had become important to me.

He and I always met out. A few times, he came to my apartment, but I had never been to his house (either of them). I knew about them, though. He had a two-bedroom cabin in the woods about forty-five minutes outside of town near Ridley Creek State Park. He loved nature and he went fishing and hiking there.

Sometimes, he would leave my apartment at ten o'clock at night and go spend the night at his other house so that he could wake up in the country and enjoy it out there for the first few hours of the day. He called it his "camp" and always spoke humbly of his things but I had seen pictures and it was a dream cabin in the woods. I hadn't been to his apartment in the city, either. I knew exactly what building it was in, and I knew that it was, no doubt, gorgeous. I just never went there.

I always suggested going to my place. I had a roommate, and Eric lived alone. If I went to his place and we had a ton of time alone in his gorgeous home, it might prove to be too much temptation.

I was happy with how slowly we had been taking things—right up until the end of January when it was time for him to go to Los Angeles to the Grammy Awards. I had completely forgotten about it, and then all of a sudden, it was upon us.

He offered to cancel his plans back when we were at Uncle E's. I had told my Aunt Rhonda about him going before Eric made it to Lexington, and she brought it up with him over dinner one night. He asked me afterward if I had any feelings about it, and I did what anyone else would do. I lied. I assured him that I didn't care at all—that I wanted him to go—that it made me feel important to know someone who was going to music's biggest night.

I regretted going so far as to encourage him to go, but that was what I did at the time. I put it out of my head and forgot about it right up until it was time for him to leave for California.

I hated the thought of Eric leaving. I was jealous of anyone and everyone who so much as checked him out as he walked by. I was extremely protective of the beautiful budding relationship we had. I didn't, however, show him any of these emotions. I acted confident and happy for him even though I was worried and disconcerted about it.

He left Saturday morning and would be back on Monday. The Grammys would take place on Sunday afternoon/evening. We texted back-and-forth several times on Saturday, and then he called me Sunday morning. He had gone out with some of his LA friends the night before, and he told me a few of the highlights. I had hung out with my friends, as well, and we swapped stories.

Eric had gone to a venue where there was big band music and swing dancing. Elle Wallace was with him. He didn't try to hide it. There were other people, too, but she was there. She was the friend he went to see, so it didn't surprise me that they hung out. But it didn't make it any easier for me to hear about it the following morning.

Ultimately, I had to trust him. If I couldn't trust him then there was no reason for me to give him my heart in the first place. We talked for a good while on Sunday—almost an hour. Eric called at 1pm my time. It was still morning for him. He told me about his plans for the award show that evening and how, with the red carpet and the after party and everything, he probably wouldn't talk to me again until the following day. I easily agreed, saying that I was surprised to have heard from him at all considering how busy he must be.

I made some art after I hung up with Eric that day. Other than the occasional addition of watercolor to one of my drawings, I was not usually a big painter. But I felt like painting that day. I had to go to the store to get a canvas and some acrylics, but it was a small price to pay for the enjoyment I got out of the project.

I had a good time. I played pop music and made still life paintings of fun things like candy and ice cream cones and toys. I was thankful I bought a three-pack of canvases because I ended up working on all three of them. With drying time, it would probably take me a few days to completely finish them, but all three canvases were officially works in progress, and all of them made me smile.

I took a break Sunday evening to have dinner at my mom's house, but I came back and worked on the paintings again until later that night. I also made a couple of lucky cups while I was waiting for paint to dry. I missed Eric, but I felt better when I was being creative and focused while he was gone. It had been a productive day.

It was midnight, and I was in my bedroom watching a historical series about Vikings when I got a call from Eric.

I had been just about to doze off, so I cleared my throat and did my best to make myself sound alert when I picked up the phone. "Hello?"

I heard music in the background the instant I put the phone to my ear. It was loud—a heavy funk rhythm. I heard rustling of the phone.

"Hello?" I repeated.

"He-hello, this… is this… this is Elle, who is this?"

"This is Olivia," I said, somewhat guarded.

It was noisy on the other end, and I could tell just by the sound and the fluctuation of her voice that she was partying.

"I hadta make sure you exist," she said. "Yeah, she's on the phone. Here she is, right here. I'm talking to her."

She was talking to someone else when she said that because she yelled it away from the phone.

"Oh my ge-oish. Eric Strauss likes you too much," she said, speaking closer to the phone again in a whiny tone.

"Me?" I asked even though that was obvious.

"Olivia this, and Olivia that," she said, not answering my question. "I don't know what you did to him but you broke him. It's so annoying. Annoying that he won't kiss me anymore. Just as friends, even. I used to do that with Eric. Kiss and stuff. I had to make sure you exist so I know he's not just blowing me off. Hey, it's truuue!"

Pause.

"I'm talking to Eric's girlfriend right now. Philadelphia. Yeah. Right now. On the phone. Seriously. You wanna talk to her? Come with me to peeeee."

She was inebriated, I could tell that by the way she spoke. I listened closely, trying to distinguish her confusing words over the loud music while feeling a little sick to my stomach. It seemed like she was asking someone if they wanted to talk to me, which was crazy since I didn't think Eric was the person she was talking to. I wondered where he was during all of this.

Elle giggled with a high-pitched squeal. "Stoooop!" she said, still talking to someone else. "Okay, I'm getting off. (Some rustling.) Hey, don't tell him I called you, kay, byeeee!" She spoke quickly and in a sing-song voice that made me cringe. She must have been talking to me because seconds later, she hung up.

I set the phone down on the bed next to me, feeling stiff, like this whole phone call had been a dream.

Girlfriend.

Of all the things she said, and some I'd like to forget, the word girlfriend was what rang in my mind. She called me Eric's girlfriend. I couldn't hear her that well, but I heard that word plain as day.

Eric and I hadn't talked about that. He had never said that word to or about me before. Half of me was furious to get a phone call like that where a stranger talked about kissing Eric, and the other half of me was overjoyed that she said he wouldn't do it anymore. Plus, she used the word girlfriend about me.

The whole conversation, if you want to call it that, was maybe only about two minutes long, but I kept replaying it until I fell asleep.

She definitely said they used to kiss.

It shouldn't surprise me that Eric had a past. We weren't fourteen anymore, after all. I knew that he had kissed other women just like I had kissed other guys. It wasn't a big deal that he kissed this particular woman, either. I would start to feel upset that he was there in LA with her now, but then I would remember how I had encouraged him to go. I had those types of back-and-forth thoughts before I fell asleep.

I woke up at 8am with Eric on my mind.

Lately, I had been trying to start my day with a prayer. I didn't pray for a long time or anything, I just recited the Lord's prayer and then listed some things I was thankful for and maybe said some things I could use a little help with. I wanted to pick up my phone when I opened my eyes, but I made myself pray first.

Eric was on my mind, so I talked to God about him. I didn't necessarily want to forbid him from doing cool things in his life, but I also didn't enjoy sending him off to LA. I asked God to give me a clear feeling about Eric—to help me know if he was the one who should be in my life. I laid there for a minute or two, thinking, considering, praying, hoping.

I grabbed my phone, wishing it would start ringing so I could hear Eric's voice. I turned it on and I blinked at the words on the screen.

The first thing I saw was Eric's name, and I smiled knowing it was a text from him. I blinked the sleep out of my eyes so that I could focus on the words.

Eric:

I know it's really late where you are. I just needed to tell you I miss you. I wish you were here with me. I want to talk to you. I want you next to me. I hope you're dreaming about me right now. I'll see you tomorrow.

My heart raced as I went to the beginning to read it again. I glanced at what time it had come in and saw that it had come in at 2:43am.

I smiled as I read it again.

I started to text him back and tell him that I missed him too and that I couldn't wait to see him, but then I remembered that it was currently 5am over there so I decided to wait.

It was at work a few hours later when I sent a text to him.

Me:

I miss you too! I can't wait to see you.

Chapter 16

I got a call back as soon as I sent a text to Eric.

"Hey," he said when he heard me pick up the phone.

"Hey yourself," I said even though I had never in my life said that phrase. I felt equally cool and dorky when it came out of my mouth.

"I thought you'd be working," he said. There was a smile in his voice.

"I am. I was. I'm just leaving to go on lunch break. Where are you?"

"Heading to meet the driver and then off to the airport. I almost went to lunch with Alec Stone."

"Nu-uh!" I said. "How? When?"

"He's friends with Jimmy. They ran into each other last night and decided to have lunch today."

"Why aren't you going?"

"It would have set my trip back three or four hours, and I'd rather not do that to the pilot. And besides, I need to get home. I have somebody waiting for me over there."

"Who?" I asked. It was a genuine question. I thought for a second that he had a meeting. Plus, I was distracted by a coworker who was waving at me as I walked down the hall toward the elevators.

"Who," Eric said, sounding sarcastic. "Who do you think I'm anxious to see, Olivia?"

"Me?" I asked after a few seconds hesitation.

"Yes, you." The certainty in his voice made me blush.

I smiled and gave a nod to a janitor who was in the elevator when I stepped onto it. I noticed the button for the first floor was already pushed, so I leaned against the wall. Eric just said he skipped lunch with Alex Stone to get home to me, and I felt like I wanted to melt because of it.

"I'm in the elevator," I announced, like a big goober.

"Are you having lunch at Roxy's, or at home?"

I didn't go home every day for lunch, and Eric knew that. It was just far enough away that I was only able to be there for fifteen minutes or so before needing to head back. I walked home frequently when the weather was nice, but not so much in the winter.

"I'm going home today," I said, answering Eric's question. "Jillian called and asked if I would go by there."

"To see if she left the curling iron plugged in?" Eric asked.

It was a running joke that Jillian had OCD about checking her hair styling tools and often had to turn around from where she was headed or call and ask me to go to her room and do it. It was rare that she asked me to leave work to do it, but today had been one of those days.

"The burner," I said. "She made herself a cup of tea when she came home for lunch, and she can't remember if she turned the burner off. She thought I might be going home when she called. I told her I didn't mind."

"Be careful," he said.

He cared about me, I could hear it in his tone.

"I will," I promised.

The elevator came to a stop and I gave a quick grin to the janitor before exiting ahead of him. Eric had said nothing about Elle calling me the night before. I figured there was a chance he had no idea.

"What time do you get home?" I asked as I headed toward the front doors of the building.

"I think we'll land before five," he said. "It'll take at least thirty minutes to get there from the airport at that time of day. I'll just plan on meeting you at your place after work if you want."

"That sounds amazing," I said.

***

I left work five minutes early that afternoon because I wanted to try to get home and shower before Eric came over. I wasn't dirty or sweaty, but it had been a busy day at work, and with going home for lunch, I had taken three walks—four by the time I got home.

Eric had been doing things like going to the Grammys and getting lunch invitations with Alec Stone. I figured the least I could do was shower. It had been a cold, gray day and it was already dark outside when I left work.

I stopped in the lobby so that I could prepare myself for the walk. I tightened the belt on my wool coat and pulled the hood up over my head. I had already put on a knitted hat with a pom-pom and I had to shift and wiggle a little to make my hood fit over it.

The last thing I did was put on my gloves. I stared out the windows, pulling on my gloves and absentmindedly looking through the glass door at a lady in a plaid coat who was walking by.

I had just started walking toward the door to make my way out when I heard his voice.

"Olivia."

It was my name, plain as day, and I knew it was Eric who said it. My head whipped around, and there he was. Mister Hollywood himself. I was in the building's lobby and he stood in the doorway that led to Roxy's, smiling and tilting his head playfully at me.

"What are you doing?" I asked, staring at him with wide eyes.

"I've been standing here, thinking you were going to turn and see me. I thought you would come in for something warm on your way out."

I glanced into Roxy's. Two people were behind the counter, Brandon and Carly, and both of them were looking our way. Eric had come to the shop twice while I was working, but no one had any idea that we had been seeing each other. Everyone assumed he had come by to talk to me about the lucky cup promotion. This time, however, I wasn't even working at Roxy's, and Eric had run into the lobby to catch me on my way out. Brandon and Carly were obviously curious about it.

I barely spared them a glance, though. My gaze went straight back to Eric. I had missed him something awful. I wanted to run into his arms. He was dressed with that casual sharpness I had come to love. Jeans with a casual shirt and a sporty jacket. He had on a baseball cap today. I had seen him in a cap a few other times, and I loved how it looked on him. This one was a worn-out cap with a vintage-looking Knicks logo. He was perfect.

"What are you doing here?" I asked. My hood was pushing my hat down over my eyes, and I tilted my head upward and reached up to push my hat back.

"Come inside," he said, grinning.

"Really?" I asked a bit stiffly.

"Yes. Why not? I can get you something free."

"Yeah, but I work here," I said, quietly enough that I had no chance of being overheard. "If you get me something for free, my coworkers will notice. They might think you're showing favoritism."

He stared at me. "I *am* showing favoritism," he said, unrepentantly. "You're clearly my favorite."

I smiled and shook my head at how irresistible he was. He urged me with a flick of his head to follow him inside and I did.

We had no work uniforms at Roxy's.

Our aprons were one of a kind as well. There was a lady who made them all. We got to choose a style and fabric, and she sewed them. For thirty dollars, we could buy more than one from her and have options. Brandon had on all black with a black apron like he always wore. This was a stark contrast to Carly, in her vintage inspired, knee-length, full-skirted, brightly patterned dress and ruffled apron. She looked like she was about to star in a movie set in the fifties.

"Hey Olivia," she said as we crossed the dining room headed toward the counter. It was fairly busy in there, but Brandon and Carly weren't helping customers at the moment, and there were open spots at the counter.

"Hey," I said, heading that way. I was friends with Carly. I worked the Saturday morning shift with her, and we always got along great. I didn't, however, tell her I had been seeing Eric. I could see the curiosity in her expression as we approached. He and I crossed to sit at the counter. I took off my gloves and hood, but I left on my hat and coat since I didn't think we were staying.

"That flyer went up about the lucky cups," Carly said. She nudged her chin to the register where Janet's flier was posted on a stand, and I glanced over there, smiling.

"I know, it's cool. I'm excited."

"Who knew those lucky cups would become a thing?" she said.

"I did," Eric said.

I smiled at him, and he reached out and pulled the stool out for me. I sat down, but I was a little stiff about it since it was a very chivalrous move on his part.

"Thank you," I said as I sat.

Brandon was nervous around Eric, and he went to work, wiping and scrubbing.

"What can I get you?" Carly asked, seeming more confident and comfortable than Brandon.

"I'll have some green tea," I said.

She nodded. "Steamed milk?"

"Please."

Carly went to work making my drink. I wondered why she wasn't offering to make Eric something, but then I realized there was a drink sitting in front of him. I wondered how long he had been sitting there and what he did when he saw me walking through the lobby.

Carly must have been having the same thoughts I was because she said, "I was wondering why Eric ran over there to catch you, but then Brandon reminded me about the lucky cups. At first, I thought maybe he thought you were supposed to be working tonight."

"I knew she wasn't working tonight," Eric said. "I knew she was getting off work upstairs. I was trying to catch her before she left the building."

Carly nodded and began steaming milk for my tea. I saw him look at me from the corner of my eye, so I glanced his way. That cap was too much. It caused a shadow to fall over his eyes, but they still sparkled. He was masculine and handsome. I was so relieved to see him. I was in over my head. I got lost staring at him. He was staring at me, too. He shifted on his barstool, and when he did our knees made contact.

"I, uh, have to talk to you. Do you have a minute? It's about doing that series of cups. I wanted to discuss… cup… stuff... with you."

"Sure," I said, trying not to smile. "Do you mean now?"

Carly discreetly slid a cup of tea my way, and I glanced at her with a thankful expression, trying to seem casual. "Thank you," I said to her, adding to my fake nonchalance.

A group of about four customers had just come to the door and were in the process of walking up to the register. I was thankful they were there to distract Carly and Brandon. I could smell Eric, for goodness sake. His hand was propped on the counter, and I stared at the side of it—at the light dusting of hair that grew in perfect patches on the backside of his hand. *Perfect patches of hand hair? What in the world was I thinking? How was it possible to be attracted to every little thing about someone?*

Suddenly, Eric shifted and got to his feet, clearing his throat. "I'll just talk to you about it right now," Eric said. "They've got customers out here so let's just step into the office for a minute."

He was talking to me, but he was obviously saying it for the benefit of Carla and Brandon.

"Sure," I said, getting to my feet with a businesslike nod.

Chapter 17

The tension was so thick you could cut it with a knife. I never understood that phrase before, but I got it now. In those moments as Eric and I gathered our things and headed back toward the office, the air between us was charged—it was thick with tension and attraction.

He touched me a couple of times while we walked along the counter, behind the customers, and toward the hallway that would lead us to the offices. As we moved, I realized that my body was alive with some kind of electrical feeling. The office was a large shared space with an L-shaped desk in the corner that everyone considered to be Belinda's. There was also a couch and armchair off to one side, and a small table with two chairs. That was where I had sat to do my job interview.

Eric took my hand as soon as we went through the threshold to the office. He moved around me, taking the tea out of my hand and setting it on a nearby bookshelf. He was empty handed and making good use of all his extremities. He set down my tea while at the same time kicking the door closed with his foot.

In one fluid motion, he took me over to the desk and turned me in his arms. He positioned himself leaning against the desk, propping most of his weight onto the top of it as he pulled me close. He hadn't let go of me since we entered the room. He drew me near, cradling me, one arm behind my head the other behind my waist. Eric gazed at me like I was something precious to him. He held me the way I wanted to be held, which was pretty much magical to experience.

He ducked his head, shifting so that he could bury his nose in my neck. He took a long breath in through his nose, and there was nothing I could do but smile because I knew he was sniffing me—smelling me.

He pulled back, shifting, holding me with both arms around my waist and looking straight at me. His cap had popped up while he had his face buried, and he took a second to readjust it.

"Hi," I said, since we were finally alone.

"Hello, Olivia."

"You're here."

"I am."

"And we're at Roxy's," I said.

"Yep. And I didn't really want to talk to you about promotional items."

"You didn't?" I asked faking surprise.

"No." He stared at me. "I just want to talk to you, look at you, say hello to you without everybody looking at us."

I glanced down at my chest, at the fact that he was holding me close. "This is some hello," I said.

"What did you do while I was away?" he asked, staring at me and looking content and curious.

"I painted with acrylics, which I never do. I had to go to the craft store to buy paint and canvases. I went to my mom's, too, and I made a couple of lucky cups, and different things like that, but I painted a lot."

"What'd you paint?"

"Summer-y looking stuff. Fun stuff. Toys and popsicles. I did these cool color schemes with pastels but also dark blues and purples. I painted some of the popsicles in a plastic tube, do you remember those?"

Eric nodded. "I do," he said, gazing at me, looking at my mouth, making my heart pound. "I want to see your popsicle painting."

"I did three of them. They're not quite done. I'm still adding layers and finishing touches."

"Three paintings?"

I nodded. "I saw you on TV," I said.

"You watched?"

"Not the whole show," I said. "But I had it on in the background and I looked for you enough that I found you in the crowd." I gazed at his face. "You were handsome. I was proud of you," I said, slowly. "Was it fun?"

He nodded. "It was pretty good," he said. "I saw a bunch of famous people. If that does it for you, then it was great."

"That is pretty cool," I said.

"I wish I was watching you paint," he said.

I smiled and shook my head. "No, you don't. That would be boring compared to what you did."

"It would not," he said with a completely serious expression. "I'm tired. I would love to go lay on your couch while you paint a popsicle."

"If you're on my couch, I would probably want to paint *you* and not a popsicle," I said.

"Let's go do that right now," he said, completely serious.

I grinned at him. I glanced at the door, which was still cracked.

"Don't worry about them," he said.

"How can't I? I work here. What if they come back here?"

"They won't," he said. "And, so what if they do? I'm their boss, remember? Just don't work here if it's awkward for you."

"Yeah, but I like it," I said. "I like the spending money and the free cup of coffee every day."

"If it's about money or free coffee, then quit and I will give those things to you. I'll hire you to paint popsicles for me. If you want to work here, I won't ask you to stop, but people are just going to have to get used to seeing us together. I'm not trying to come in here and pretend to talk to you about lucky cups. I missed you too much for that."

Eric saying he missed me made me think about his trip, which made me think of Elle and our phone conversation.

"Your friend called me," I said.

"Who?" his eyebrows furrowed, and his expression made it seem like he was a little jealous—like he thought it was a guy who called me.

"Elle," I said.

"Elle? When?"

"Last night," I said. "I wasn't even going to mention it. I probably shouldn't have. It was no big deal."

"Wait, when did she call you?"

"Last night," I repeated.

"I know, but how? From my phone? And when?"

I shrugged. "It wasn't too late. I think you were still hanging out with her. It was loud and there was music and everything. It might've been something going on after the show."

"How did she call you?" he asked.

"From your phone."

Eric made a contemplative, frustrated face as he slowly ducked his head and switched his hat from forward-facing to backwards. I didn't expect for him to do that, and I held back a grin at the sight. He looked gorgeous in a backwards hat and the best part about it was that he did it because he was feeling irritated and speechless about his friend calling me.

"Tell me exactly what she said to you," he said once his hat was settled in its new position.

"She just said that she wanted to call to make sure I exist. She sounded like she was partying.

There was definitely a lot of music. She was talking to someone else in the background."

"I'm really sorry about that," he said. "Did it wake you up?"

"No. And it was no big deal. She told me not to tell you she did it, so don't mention it to her."

"She said that? She told you not to tell me she called you?"

"Yes," I said with a reassuring smile, "But it's honestly not worth you mentioning it to her. Seriously, I'd rather you not."

He adjusted, making his arms comfortable around me and not caring one bit that someone could possibly come into the room and catch us.

"Did you have any sort of feelings about it?" Eric asked. "Did it make you mad at me?" He brought his hand to the back of my head again, cradling it, staring at me. His fingers were on the back of my head and his thumb played absentmindedly on my cheek.

"I wasn't mad," I said. "I mean, I got jealous a little bit, but not mad."

"You were jealous?" he asked, his mouth curving upward slightly.

I stared at him unashamedly. He was completely irresistible in that backward baseball cap. "Yes, I was jealous," I said. "But I figured if I can't trust you then what am I doing liking you, anyway? And if you're going to try to mess around, it's better that I figure it out now."

"Oh, really, so how'd I do?" he asked, his white teeth flashing at me when he smiled.

"You tell me," I said. "I wasn't there."

His eyes stayed locked on mine for a few silent seconds. He leaned against the desk, pulling me close, looking at me. "I thought about you the entire time, Olivia Tanner. You never left my mind. I could not get you out of my head, even when I tried."

"Good," I said. "I guess that means you didn't have any time for girlfriends in California."

"No, I didn't," he replied.

He ducked and brought his mouth near mine—so close that I thought he was going to kiss me. But he didn't. He hesitated, enjoying almost-kissing me.

"Are we going to get caught in here?" I whispered, wanting so badly to kiss him but feeling nervous and giddy.

"You know it wouldn't matter if we did," he said. "It's one of the perks of owning the place. I can't get in trouble."

"Even for this?" I asked.

"Even for this." He paused, and I thought he was about to do it, but he said my name instead. "Olivia."

"Yes?"

"I feel impatient." He was speaking softly, sweetly, his lips next to mine.

"You don't seem impatient," I said.

"I am though. I want you next to me every second. Is that too much to ask?"

He ducked and kissed me, a quick, soft, sticky kiss that had me stretching up, pressing myself toward him. We kissed again, several times, and an electric pulse stabbed through my lower abdomen at the feel of his lips. He pulled back enough to break contact but he left his face right next to mine.

"Can we just be together?" he asked. "Where we don't have to hide it or go slow?"

He waited for my answer, and what else was I supposed to say but, "Yes."

"Are you my girl now?" he asked. "Can I just have you from now on?"

"Yes," I said, without even making him define exactly what he meant by that.

He situated his arms again, pulling me closer and making himself comfortable. He was wearing a contented smile that made me squeeze him.

"I'm sorry you were jealous," he said.

"I told you to go," I returned.

"That was the last one," he said. "Unless it's with you. Nothing happened with me and Elle, it's just, it didn't feel right being anyone else's date."

"It didn't feel right to me either," I said. "I wasn't mad, but I wished I saw you in that tux and not her."

"You wanna see me in a tux?" he asked.

"Yes."

"It's in my bag. But it's all wrinkled. You'll probably have to wait until it's back from the cleaners."

"Do you have your own tux? You didn't just rent one?"

"No. I have one."

"Where are your bags?"

"Adrian took them to my apartment after he dropped me off here."

"So, you don't have a driver?"

"No. I was planning on going with you to your place."

"Good," I said. "I can draw you laying on my couch."

"That sounds like a magical evening." He kissed me. "Do you have food? Because if not, I'm grabbing a sandwich before we leave here."

"Food from here is definitely better than anything I have at my apartment," I said. "But it's whatever you're in the mood for. We can get something here or stop on the way home."

We were all cozy in each other's arms and discussing dinner options when the door opened. Brandon was suddenly standing in the doorway, stunned, gawking at us with wide eyes. I could tell catching us like that was the furthest thing from his mind, and he had to stand there and compute what he was seeing.

"There was… someone was asking for… a, uh… the thing you use to apply for a job—an application… yes… someone was… I, you know what, I can, uh, come back another time—"

I tried to step out of Eric's grasp, put he held me there. It didn't take much effort because I wasn't really trying to leave. I needed the comfort and reassurance of his arms while Brandon was standing there staring at us like that.

"Just come in and get it. You're not bothering us," Eric said, calmly.

Brandon stepped inside and began digging in a drawer, trying not to look at us. "I'll be in and out," he said.

We had untangled a little bit, but Eric's arms were still casually resting on me.

"Brandon, Olivia and I are seeing each other, now," Eric said.

Brandon nodded and Eric kept speaking.

"I don't know if she'll continue working here or not. She's going to do some advertising for us. It's up to her if she still wants to work up front. Just know that she's with me. I'll let Belinda know, too, but Olivia's got an open tab."

"Yes, of course," Brandon said, bowing a little at us. "And a lovely choice," he said, his voice shaking a little. "Olivia's great," he added, clarifying.

"I know, and thank you," Eric said.

"Thank *you*," Brandon said, still nervous. He held the job application in his hand and he waved at us with it before turning to walk out. It was surreal, standing next to Eric and seeing how people looked at him. He really was the boss around here.

"Are you two ordering anything from the kitchen?" Brandon asked, glancing over his shoulder.

"Yeah, actually, we'll take a couple of sandwiches to go. We'll stop by the kitchen on our way out."

"Can I get something started for you?"

Eric looked at me as if telling me to make the call, and I shook my head almost imperceptibly.

"We can do it," I said.

"We can do it," Eric said, repeating my words as he shifted to look at Brandon.

He gave us a smile and nod before turning to walk away.

Chapter 18

A month later

I got closer and closer to Eric as the weeks passed. He was my boyfriend and I was his girlfriend, and we spent as much time together as possible—getting comfortable in each other's lives. We met one another's parents and friends, we went out to dinner and social outings, and watched movies snuggled-up on the couch. We went for walks and talked into the middle of the night. We did all the things couples do.

I continued to work at Roxy's twice a week, but it wasn't a big deal. People asked me about it, but their curiosity was quenched after a few short questions and answers. I liked all of my coworkers there, and none of them treated me any differently, for better or for worse, when they heard I was dating Eric.

He loved the lucky cup promotion. He thought it was a genius idea, and he thanked me multiple times for coming up with it. My lucky cups had gotten more detailed and intricate than the ones I used to whip up before a shift at the coffee shop. I had to step up my game with the promotion and everything.

Eric stepped up with the rules, too.

The distribution was fair and mapped-out so that employees couldn't be tempted to offer it to a friend. A lucky cup, when redeemed, was worth a hundred dollars cash and a Roxy's t-shirt. It was part of the promotion. You could take your lucky cup to the roasting house on North 57th Street and trade it for a hundred dollars. And since it was just doodling on a paper cup and not a fine piece of art, it was a no brainer that people would turn it in.

Most of them took pictures with it and then turned it in for the prize within a few days. In the weeks since they had been introduced, most of them had been redeemed, but a few were still MIA. Several of my old ones had been turned in, too, which was also part of the deal.

There had been more than two weeks of the promotion so far, and it was fun to check the hashtag each day on social media and see if anyone posted. People had taken some artistic photographs with their lucky cup, and I loved having my little art piece featured in someone else's creativity.

Everything regarding the promotion was wonderful.

Until 3:52pm on a random Friday afternoon.

I was about to get off of work.

My boss, Janet, had just come into my office space. She said for me to meet her in her office in five minutes—that she wanted to give me a few notes about next week's projects so that I could be thinking about them. She told me I was free to leave for the day after that.

I wrapped up what I was doing and gathered my things. I had plans for dinner with Eric and his family that evening, and I was happy to go home a little early and start getting ready.

Just before I went to Janet's office, I glanced at my phone to see if Eric had called or texted. He hadn't, but that didn't surprise me. I had already talked to him on my lunch break, and I knew he had plans to pick me up at 6:30.

While I had my phone out, I looked at Instagram. I searched the hashtag #roxysluckycup so frequently that it came up as soon as I pressed the search bar.

There were a few new entries, and I smiled as I stared down at the photos.

I clicked on the first one to enlarge it. It was a photo of a woman with her cup in one hand and a homemade sign that said *winner-winner-chicken-dinner* in fancy, handwritten script.

I was smiling at that one until I scrolled far enough to focus on the next photo.

It was a split-screen photo with two images in one. The photos were zoomed-in on various parts of the cup with red circles superimposed on the screen like they were pointing certain things out. I scrolled down and read the comment.

So, I got a lucky cup at Roxy's Coffee on Cottman Avenue today, and honestly, guys, meh. Meh is being generous. This cup is okay at best. I was thrilled when I realized I had been chosen as a winner of Roxy's lucky cup promotion, but then I was immediately underwhelmed by what I had been given. The art itself, while being hand drawn and one of a kind, looks to have been done by an eighth grader. The experience as a whole was pretty good, and with a little more effort by art department at Roxy's, it could be a great concept. The full breakdown of my experience with a #roxysluckycup along with more photos can be found on my blog. Link in bio.

I finished reading that caption, feeling a bit like I was in a dream—a nightmare. How and why was someone taking time out of their day to write such hurtful things? I felt actual heat fill my chest and rise up my neck and into my head. I blushed, and not the good kind where my cheeks turned pink and I looked pretty. This was the kind where I knew my whole face was red. The kind where I had to sit down and cool off for a minute.

I felt hurt by her words, and while I knew I shouldn't go to her bio and follow the link to her blog, that was the first thing I did. My face was flaming hot as the website opened and I stared at close-up photos of my own work.

She wrote a whole essay on her experience, detailing what the barista was wearing and what he said when he handed her the cup. She talked about what the coffee tasted like and everything. I tried to scan those parts because I knew Janet would be expecting me in her office. The blog entry was longer than I thought it would be, and I didn't have time to read it all. I didn't want to read it all.

I scanned until I found the paragraphs where she tore my drawing apart—ripped it to shreds. My flaws were stated in detail.

The shading is off.
These lines... what are they connecting to? All of the line work needs to be thinner.
Who draws a hand like this?
This character is too top heavy. How would she even walk? She would topple over. Bad character design.
Unrealistic, uninspired.
I am left feeling underwhelmed.
Sorry, but this lucky cup was a lucky flunk. Thank God I get a hundred bucks out of the deal because otherwise I would be mad at Roxy's for making me go through the trouble of winning.

I read all the words that detailed the things I had done wrong. I looked at the corresponding photos—things she had circled. And by the end of it, I kind of agreed with her. I could see what she was talking about with the line work. Maybe the rabbit character *was* too top heavy.

That cup had been one of my favorites when I put it out, and now it was officially my most hated cup I had ever done. It was my most hated drawing ever.

Why was I drawing lucky cups anyway? I hadn't meant for them to be a part of a big a promotion. This was Eric's idea, not mine. I hadn't meant for there to be fliers. Drawing on cups was just something I enjoyed. I wanted to give them to regular customers and friends. People who enjoyed them for what they were worth—people who might just get a smile out of finding a drawing on their coffee cup. I never dreamed I would have my work picked apart on someone's blog. Was it even okay for her to do that? Was it considered slander? Could I make her pull it down off of the internet? Could I, at least, pull that post off of Instagram?

My mind began racing with different ways to defend myself—to make this whole thing go away.

Emotions flooded through me as I read and re-read some of the things she wrote. It was humiliating. She was telling everyone on the whole internet that the lucky cups at Roxy's royally sucked, and there was nothing I could do about it.

She wrote well. She sounded intelligent and convincing, and she was sarcastic and funny, only it was at my expense and the pain of it was physical. I felt an unpleasant, hot, gushing, rushing sensation that made me feel ill. I was nauseous and light headed. It was definitely a panic attack. I had experienced them before and I knew what they felt like. But that didn't stop me from feeling like I was about to die. I wanted to lie on the floor, right there in my cubical.

Eric would, no doubt, see this and figure out that the whole lucky cup thing was a bust. I felt, in an odd way, like this could disrupt our relationship—possibly end it. Dread, fear, hurt, embarrassment, anger. All of these things throbbed and pulsed through my body.

I was in a complete daze as I dropped my phone into my purse and went into Janet's office. I was on autopilot during the short meeting with my boss, but I made it through without her noticing that I was distracted. I was distracted, though. I was sick with it. I could not wait to get home so that I could just break down and cry.

I left Stone Lion, feeling woozy and sick to my stomach. I called Eric on my way home and told him I had gotten sick at work and wouldn't be able to make it to dinner. He was worried about me and offered to come over and take care of me, but I insisted that it was something I ate and that I wanted to just go home and go to bed.

It was a rough night for me.

Those hours were full of doubt, hurt, fear, and embarrassment. It truly did seem like the end of the world—at least the end of my world as I knew it.

Lucky cups were supposed to be happy. I had no idea how I was supposed to be happy and produce something joyful when I knew there were people out there who would judge me so harshly.

Then I made the mistake of going back to the post. I guess I was hoping it would disappear. All I found was the devastating news that other people had *liked* it. Multiple people had actually reached out and pressed the *like* button on all of the mean things she said about me. In fact, her post had more likes then a lot of the others under the *Roxy's lucky cup* hashtag. It caused me to experience an odd sort of hurt, seeing those likes coming from people who didn't know me. *How could other people encourage her to be mean to me? What in the world had happened? I thought I was just putting something fun and positive into the world, and all I felt was attacked.*

I wallowed in a sea of self-doubt and self-pity all evening.

Eric texted me, and I gave him all the right answers to make him think I was fine but still dealing with food poisoning.

I was scheduled to work my shift at Roxy's at 8am the following morning. I went back and forth about whether or not I was going to call in sick. I had taken scheduled days off, but I had never called in sick at the last minute, and I knew my story could match what Eric already thought was the truth.

I was restless and I woke up at 6am not knowing whether or not I would call in sick. There were multiple reasons for me to go.

For starters, I knew I had to go on with my life. It simply wasn't an option to quit going to work and functioning for the rest of my life.

Also, I wanted to go to make sure nobody was talking about it.

The worry of it all had actually caused me to feel sick, though, so I physically didn't feel like going.

I called and talked to Carly who took the message. She gave her well-wishes and said they'd work on finding someone to replace me for my shift.

Chapter 19

I spent my morning watching a dramatic series on television that was set in medieval times. I watched two-and-a-half episodes, and I barely followed the storyline because the whole time, my thoughts were consumed with blogs and social media posts.

I was generally a positive person, and I hated feeling discouraged and sad. I cried a lot last night, but this morning, I was doing a little better. I had a good cry after I called in sick to work, but I had been able to keep from doing it while I watched television.

It was just after 10am when I got a call from Eric.

I answered on the second ring.

I knew if my voice was puny, it would only reinforce my lie. "Hello?"

"How are you?" he asked.

"Better than last night," I said, since it was the truth.

"I thought you were going to try to go to work this morning."

We had talked about it the night before when I called him to tell him I couldn't go to dinner. I told him it wasn't that bad and I was sure I'd be right as rain in the morning.

"I debated on going this morning, but I wasn't quite there yet," I said.

"Can I please come over and see you? Bring you something? Soup? Popsicles?"

"No, no, you don't need to do that. Thank you. How was the Annabella last night?" (That was where we were supposed to eat.)

"It was fine. Good. I was worried about you."

"Oh, I'm sorry," I said. "I'm fine."

"You don't sound fine."

"I am. I'm just out of it. I was just sitting here, watching a movie."

"Can I come watch it with you?" he asked.

"Yes."

I wanted to deny him. I wanted to be alone and shut out everyone and everything, but I couldn't get the word no to come out of my mouth when it came to Eric. He asked me if he could come over and watch a movie with me, and the only logical answer to that was yes.

***

Eric knocked on the door of my apartment thirty minutes later with grocery bags in hand. He had stopped for a sick care package with popsicles, soup and crackers, and a few different drink options.

He was everything I ever dreamed of, which in my fragile state, was somehow a bad thing.

He was definitely too good for me.

Those stupid cups were an embarrassment.

I struggled with those types of thoughts while he was sitting right next to me, watching television. My roommate was in the living room with her boyfriend, so Eric and I had come into my bedroom to continue that series I had been watching. We were both sitting on the bed with our backs propped against pillows. I was under the covers and he was on top. He had kicked off his shoes and was comfortable sitting next to me in jeans and a t-shirt with socks.

"How about a popsicle?" he asked between episodes.

I nodded, and he hopped off of the bed, crossing my bedroom with athletic grace before heading into the living room. I kept the show paused for him, waiting while he was out of the room. It took him a few minutes. I heard him talking to my roommate, so I wasn't surprised. They discussed my condition and the fact that I didn't come out of my room all night. Eric came into the room a few minutes later with two popsicles. Both of them were grape, which was my favorite.

"Today's lucky cup is at your location," he said. "It might get given away on your shift. That would have been cool if you would have been there."

I didn't mean to do it, but I felt so helpless about the situation that I let out a small, cynical scoff.

"What?" he said, hearing me.

He was somewhat distracted while he pulled this popsicle out the plastic wrapper, and so was I.

"Nothing," I said. "I'm just kind of done with those cups right now."

Eric adjusted his seating position, kicking his leg up and bending his knee while turning to face me. "What'd you say?"

"Nothing. It's nothing. I just feel... a little discouraged about them." (Understatement of the year.)

"Why do you feel discouraged?" he asked.

I tried my absolute best to keep it from happening, but hot tears began stinging my eyes the instant I thought about how to answer his question. I blinked and looked away, staring at the comforter, and trying my best to keep tears from overflowing onto my cheeks. I put the popsicle into my mouth, hoping the sweet coldness would serve as a distraction. Thankfully, it did.

"Why do you feel discouraged, Olivia?" he asked, since I hadn't answered.

"There was a mean write-up about them."

"Was it something with the hashtag? Somebody complaining?"

"Yes."

"I saw that."

My gaze snapped up to meet his. "You did?"

He nodded.

"W-what'd you see?"

"Just that lady complaining about it. The one with the red circles?"

"Yes. You saw it?"

"Yes. I was hoping you wouldn't, though."

I stared at him, wondering how he thought I could miss it and why he didn't think it was a big deal.

"Can you believe someone would do that?" I asked.

"Do what?"

"Write all that stuff."

He shrugged a little, making a regretful face. "Unfortunately, it's part of it. You're not going to be able to escape people giving their opinions."

"Yeah, but it was super mean."

"Sometimes they are," he said, completely calm and levelheaded.

I put the popsicle in my mouth again but mostly to keep it from melting. They were getting soft since Eric had stopped to talk to my roommate after picking them up, and both of us took a bite for that reason. He was staring at me like he didn't understand the gravity of the situation.

"People liked and responded to what she said," I said.

"So?"

"So, don't you think that's going to have repercussions? Don't you think it means people don't like the promotion?"

"Sure it does," he said. "Some people don't like the promotion. Some people don't like Roxy's coffee at all. No matter what it is, Olivia, some people won't like it."

"Yeah, but they don't have to write about it in detail for other people to read. And who are these people that go around liking other people's meanness? That's just double mean. Why would anyone do that?"

"It's not mean. It's not personal. It's just their opinion. People are used to stating their opinion. They don't know what they're doing. They don't realize people's feelings are involved. It's just a product, and they're judging it. They have the right to judge it."

"Yeah, but it's going to make other people not want to go to Roxy's. I don't care as much for me, I mean, I do, but I'm more worried about you."

"Please don't worry about me," he said "Those kinds of things don't change anything. People know there are rants on the internet. I saw that lady's thing this morning and I didn't even think twice about it. I'm sorry if you did."

I let out a weak humorless sound that was basically a half-laugh combined with a sigh. We had been working on our popsicles as we talked and I took a slow, deep, measured breath as I took another bite. I was relieved by Eric's casual reaction to everything.

"I was so embarrassed," I said.

"Don't let it do that to you," he said.

Our popsicles were so melted that they went down quickly. We polished them off in one more bite. I set my stick onto my nightstand. Eric handed me his, and I did the same thing with it.

Eric reached out for me and took me into his arms. He leaned back against the pillows pulling me with him, holding me with my back toward his chest.

"I'm sorry," he said. "That on top of being sick."

"That's *why* I'm sick."

Eric was still and quiet for a few seconds, and then I felt him shift. The movement was small but quick, and I could tell he was trying to look at me, so I turned to focus on him.

"What do you mean?" he asked.

"I mean, that's why I don't feel good."

"You mean last night? Your food poisoning?"

"It was... internet... poisoning..." I said it slowly and dramatically like the kid on A Christmas Story when he said 'soap poisoning', and it caused Eric to start to smile, but he was still confused looking, and he shook his head.

"Are you not sick right now?"

"I mean, I guess technically my body isn't sick. But I definitely wasn't feeling right."

"From the stuff the lady said?" he asked, still looking perplexed.

"Yes."

He paused and blinked at me. "Oh, well... good," he said, seeming at a loss for words. "Because you definitely don't need to worry about that. It won't be the last time it happens, I promise."

"How am I supposed to move on? It makes me question myself. I was just trying to do it for my regular customers."

"Well, now you're doing it for more than your regular customers. You don't have control of who gets a hold of your stuff and comments on it or what they say. All you can control is how you react. If she pointed out something like *'the ink she used on the cup smeared all over my shirt,'* then you respond to that and you find better ink. But if someone is just commenting on your style, there's nothing you can or should do about that. You can't second guess yourself because of someone else's opinion. You just do what you do. Some people will like you and some people won't. You have to be yourself."

"And I guess that'll just have to be good enough," I said, feeling exponentially better. I could actually breathe easier.

"Of course it's good enough, Olivia. I didn't hire you for this project because I like you. I hired you because it's a great idea and you're great at it. Ultimately, this falls on me. You just have to trust my taste, which, as we both know, is impeccable."

I regarded him thoughtfully. "I don't know how it's possible that you could just say some words and I physically feel better."

"Why not? It was just words that made you physically feel bad in the first place."

I let out a little laugh when he said that, because he was right. "Thank you for talking to me about it," I said in a sincere tone. "I really do feel better."

"You have to be honest with me about what's going on with you," he said.

"You're right," I agreed. "I'm sorry. I was just worried that it would affect things between us."

"Well it doesn't. And you have to promise to tell me the truth from now on."

"I will. I'm so sorry I lied. I should have just told you what was going on. I wasted a whole day on this, basically."

"So, do you feel better? Because I was about to tell Ethan and Bridget that they could have our tickets for tonight."

"Oh, yeah, that's right," I said.

The 76ers were playing the Knicks tonight. Uncle E still had a ton of connections in the NBA, and knew Eric liked the Knicks, so he got us tickets.

"Come on, it's Saturday," he said.

"It is Saturday," I said, feeling like a completely different woman. "Think of the possibilities."

"Yeah, I was planning on taking you out for steak before the game."

"Oh, that was such a good plan," I said.

He shrugged. "It still is a good plan."

"Great, so let's do it," I said, casually.

"Great," he said, shrugging a shoulder. Without warning, he tackled me, rolling over me just the right way so that we ended up in a new position in the middle of the bed. This time, I was sitting up and he was lying across my lap, propped onto his hand, gloriously trapping me.

"Your mouth is going to taste like grape popsicles," he said, scanning my face. His gaze hesitated when it reached my mouth, and I smiled at him.

"That's because I just ate one," I said.

He was so close to me that I leaned in and rubbed my cheek gently on his. It was a gesture of thanks and love and tenderness.

And then I found out that all problems had a way of completely disappearing when you kiss a gorgeous man who tastes like grape popsicles.

Chapter 20

Seven months later
Late September
Elmont, NY

Belmont Park was a Thoroughbred racing facility where the Belmont Stakes were held. It was located in a place called Elmont (without the B) New York.

Mister Everything was just starting his racing career and would run at Belmont Park in a two-year-old race called the Pilgrim Stakes that weekend. The trip from Philadelphia to New York was easy in a car, but Eric and I made the fast flight to the city and took a rental car to the track. We used his father's jet. It wasn't the first time I had ridden in it since we'd been together, but I was still getting used to that sort of lifestyle.

Eric was so low-key and easy to be around that the private jet thing was still a little surreal. There was a blacked-out SUV waiting for us at the airport. Eric enjoyed driving and rarely hired drivers.

I was in the best mood.

My brother would be at the races, and I was excited to see him. Mister Everything's big race wasn't until the following day, but we booked a room in the same hotel where my brother was staying and we met up with him as soon as we made it to town. We checked into our hotel and hung out with my brother for a little while before leaving to go eat dinner.

Eric drove and Jude rode with us. I offered to let my brother sit in the front since he was bigger than me, but he insisted that he didn't mind getting in the back.

My uncle and now my brother were in the business of breeding and training horses, and because of that, I had been to my share of races. Belmont Park was close to Philadelphia, and I had been there at least five times in the past, supporting my family. It was always fun.

I liked the city and had been to several good restaurants. I hadn't been to the one we were going to tonight, but Jude had and he loved it. It was a country kitchen with things like fried chicken and cornbread and greens, and Jude had always loved that type of thing. This place served things family style where dishes are set in bowls on a table and everyone passed them around and shared. Eric and I loved home-cooking as well and we easily chose that place when Jude gave us options. It was in Brookville, though, which was a thirty-minute drive from our hotel. None of us minded. I loved seeing Jude and catching up with him.

Mister Everything and his upcoming race was the primary thing on Jude's mind, so we talked about that while we were driving. He was excited and had hopes of not just placing but winning. I hated to get my hopes up, but I sincerely wanted that to happen.

It was dark out and we were in the middle of nowhere when I heard a loud, shrill booip-booip sound from behind us. I saw blue flashing lights spill into the truck. "Booip-booip-booip," the sound was ear-piercing, and startled me every time it happened. It happened again, a third set of quick, jarring sounds.

I had turned in my seat where I could see Eric and it was easy to glance back toward Jude. I clearly saw the flashes of light coming into the vehicle from the back window.

"Were you speeding?" Jude asked, glancing over Eric's shoulder, peering at the dashboard.

Eric began slowing down. "He might just need to pass me," he murmured calmly as he began pulling over. "Hang on... just a second..." he continued, talking absentmindedly as he drove onto the shoulder.

"He's stopping behind us," Jude said, looking back, staring straight at the flashing lights. I was looking back, too.

We were doing nothing wrong and still my heart was in my throat.

"Were you speeding?" Jude asked again, glancing back.

"No," I answered even though I had no idea. It hadn't felt like we were speeding. I stared at the side of Eric's face, watching as he intently stared into the rearview mirror.

"He's getting out," Jude announced.

"I see him," Eric said calmly.

"Why do you think he's stopping us?" I asked.

I knew Jude and I should both just be quiet, but I was nervous and I couldn't help it.

"I guess we're about to find out," Eric said as he shifted to stare into side view mirror. He rolled down the driver's window, and I watched as an officer approached the vehicle. He was a huge man with a black beard and a pot belly. He walked with a swayback.

It was dark out and he shined his flashlight through the backseat window before shining it right in Eric's face. I saw Eric flinch a little as a result of the bright light, and I winced right along with him. The officer leaned down and shifted the flashlight, and suddenly the blinding light hit me in the face. I squinted, making a face. I could faintly see his outline.

"License and insurance please."

"It's a rental," Eric said.

"I know. I ran your tags. That's why I didn't ask for your vehicle registration."

He continued to shine the bright light directly on Eric's lap as he spoke. Eric had already taken his wallet out of his pocket, and he began to fish for his driver's license. He handed it to the guy.

"I don't have my car insurance policy on me," he said. "I could look it up on my phone, but I thought that was through the rental agency."

"Philadelphia," the officer said, looking at Eric's license and ignoring his statement. "What's your business in New York, exactly?"

The officer couldn't see me do it, but I glanced at Jude with a worried, annoyed expression.

"We've got a horse racing at Belmont Park tomorrow." Jude was the one who spoke. He cracked his window so that he could make that interjection, and the officer shined the light directly on Jude's face when he did.

"Sir, roll your window up. I'm talking to the driver." His tone was abrupt and no-nonsense.

Jude rolled up the window, turning to stare stiffly at me with a slightly wide-eyed expression. The officer was not in a good mood. I was on edge already, but the way he barked at Jude made me feel defensive and wary.

"Was there a problem officer?" Eric asked. "Was there a reason you pulled me over?"

"You were flying down this road," the officer said. "The speed limit on this road is fifty-five, and I clocked you at seventy."

"Oh, I definitely wasn't doing seventy," Eric said, sounding sure of himself but cautious and respectful at the same time.

The light went directly into his face. "Excuse me?" the officer said, as if daring Eric to say that again.

Eric cleared his throat. "It could be that your radar was off, but I wasn't going seventy. Not down this little two-lane."

"He wasn't speeding," I said, leaning over. "I saw."

I hadn't seen. It was a lie. But I could tell Eric was being honest, and I knew I needed to say something to reinforce our side of this story. I couldn't let him say things that weren't true.

I had a price to pay for speaking up. The police turned the flashlight directly on me again.

"Ma'am I'm speaking to the gentleman who's driving," he growled. "No more interruptions from either of you."

"I apologize, officer, but I sincerely wasn't speeding. I had just glanced at the speedometer before you pulled me over. I was going under the limit actually."

"Are you calling me a liar, son?" He stepped back, lowering the flashlight, looking at Eric man-to-man, daring him. It was intense. I could not look directly at the guy. I was scared. It was dark out and we were in the middle of nowhere. Cars passed us every so often, but we were far enough onto the shoulder that they didn't even slow down. The officer took a step back, staring us down and staring down our whole vehicle suspiciously. He reached up to his shoulder, and pressed the button to speak on the little radio that was connected to his uniform.

"This is Alpha Prescott. I've got a four-twenty-five on my hands. I'm requesting backup."

"Requesting backup?" I mouthed the words to my brother, wearing a confused expression. Eric was looking at the officer. Neither of them had seen me. Jude was as suspicious as I was.

"Video," he said. Only he was mouthing the words just like I was and I wasn't able to understand him.

I made a face to let my brother know I didn't get it.

"Vi-de-o," he mouthed the words exaggeratedly, and he also held up his phone and aimed it just the right way so that I was able to tell what he was saying.

He was telling me to video the interaction with the police. It took me a few seconds to figure out that he was telling me to do it because he was scared of that cop and thought this was about to get sketchy. A wave of fear washed over me when I realized what Jude was implying.

"You video," I said. I leaned toward him and whispered the words out loud instead of mouthing them.

The officer was talking on his radio and wasn't paying attention to me. Jude leaned over so that he could take the phone out of his back pocket. He discreetly began pushing the right buttons. I watched as he stiffly tilted the camera toward the officer.

"It's not gonna pick up what he's saying," Jude said.

I widened my eyes at him, telling him he was talking too loud. The officer concluded the radio correspondence with all of his police code and jargon. I didn't understand it, but it made me feel like he was telling the person on the other end that he thought we were guilty of something.

"Officer, if there's no other problem than the speeding, I'll go ahead and take the ticket so we can be on our way."

"I'm afraid we're way past that," he said.

Jude and I shared another annoyed glance that he couldn't see.

He pressed the button on his radio and began saying more code about having a four-twenty-five on his hands and needing backup. He was giving our location, and I automatically started glancing all around and assuming that the headlights I saw far off in the distance were cops that were heading our way.

My heart began pounding in earnest now. The surreal experience had somehow gone from being an annoyance to having me amped up and full of dread. Adrenaline coursed through my body as thirty seconds of utter chaos ensued.

Eric went to reach for something. His wallet—something in his pocket. It must have been his wallet or keys or something in his pocket because he leaned to the side and reached back in a gesture like he was going to retrieve something from his backside. The officer went ballistic. He put his hand on his gun like he was about to pull it out and start shouting. He was in a fighting stance. His knees were bent and he had one hand on his gun in one hand out toward Eric.

"I was just going to get my phone to look up my—" Eric was not speaking quietly, but the officer did not hear him for his own yelling.

The officer took his hand off of his gun holster just long enough to press the button on his radio. I heard him saying something about the suspect having a possible firearm, land the next thing I knew he was shouting for Eric to, "Get out of the car! Get out of the car!" He shouted fiercely.

Eric began moving. Those seconds were so heart pounding that it was difficult for me to understand what was going on. My brother was videoing the whole thing, and I could do nothing but sit there and watch helplessly.

I covered my face and watched through my fingers as Eric opened his door and stepped outside. The officer was shouting things like, *"Keep your hands where I can see them!"*

The door was open and I watched as the officer, poised to fight, barked orders at Eric.

"Put your hands on your head and turn around!" he yelled. Eric did as the officer said, and the guy began patting him down.

Jude and I looked at each other, both of us wearing helpless, worried expressions. I still had a hand over my face, but I knew my brother could see me—could see the panic in my eyes. Neither of us knew what to do to help.

Two huge SUV's came speeding up with their lights flashing.

"On your knees!" the officer yelled before anyone could get out of their vehicles.

Eric was facing me when the officer told him to do that and I saw his face fall in confusion. He was always so in control that I felt gut-wrenched seeing him this way. There was just no way I could let him get down on his knees like a criminal. My brother still had his phone trained on the action outside the vehicle.

I let out a, "Noooo!" but my voice was weak and it sounded distant even to my own ears.

The next thing I knew, the officer pushed Eric down by the shoulder and Eric was forced to his knees right in front of me. I watched anxiously, heart pounding, starting to panic.

"Ask her!" he growled.

I was looking straight at Eric when his hands lowered and his serious, confused expression softened. A slow grin touched the corners of his mouth. My heart was pounding in my ears in those dreamlike seconds. I watched Eric's handsome face brake into a slow smile.

"Ask her, why don't cha!" I heard someone else yell from the front side of the vehicle and I looked that way to see my father and a group of others heading our way. My father had, no doubt, been the one who yelled, I recognized his voice.

My body had a delayed reaction to realizing that nothing was wrong. It took several seconds for me to figure out what was actually going on. Those stressful moments had ended with Eric down on his knees. And there was nothing wrong. My family was here. This was a planned moment. Adrenaline was still pumping as I gazed at Eric with a confused expression.

"Olivia, would you please marry me?"

My heart was rattling in my chest, and my blood felt hot and thick as I turned and reached for the door handle. I opened the car door and got out of the vehicle, hopping to the ground and moving around the front of it, trying desperately to get to Eric.

I was so out of it that I felt like I was moving slower than normal, like my body wasn't fully cooperating. Everything felt like I was in a liquid dreamscape. I barely took in everyone who was standing around, which seemed to be about ten or twelve people, all friends and family.

It felt like it took me forever to get to Eric, and by the time I did, he was already getting to his feet. He stood just in time to take me into his arms. I was shaking and tears of relief began flooding my eyes.

"You never answered him!" someone yelled. It was a woman. I thought it might be my Aunt Rhonda. I glanced that way while I hugged Eric, and saw her standing near the cop, who was huddled up behind her. He was being so familiar that I instantly knew it was my uncle in a costume. I would have never recognized him. It wasn't a fake beard from a Halloween store. It was professionally applied stage makeup and beard. The added fake potbelly really put it over the top. Plus, he talked in a deeper voice. I would've never recognized him, even if the situation hadn't been stressful.

I could only vaguely appreciate what an elaborate plan it must have been with the lights and sirens and outfits.

"Yes!" I said, through tears.

Eric held me and kissed me, and I felt an overwhelming, surreal sense of relief, adrenaline, desire, happiness, amazement, and love. I loved this man. And in those moments of heart-pounding excitement, where everyone was gathered to celebrate, I couldn't mistake how very much he loved me too.

Epilogue

A year later

Eric and I got married in the spring, and it was now late September again. We were still newlyweds at this point which could possibly explain why we were completely inseparable. Or maybe that was just how our life would be from now on. Maybe we would just remain inseparable forever. It felt that way.

I traveled with Eric quite a bit, so I wound up quitting both of my jobs. I didn't, however, stop working. I still basically did similar job duties as I did when I was working, but now I did it as a partner of Eric's and business owner.

Now, when I went into Roxy's, I worked behind the counter or helped out some as needed, but I did it for free. I did it as someone who has an interest in the longevity of the company. I became a helper to Eric, giving opinions about the feel of the marketing. I did some of the designs myself, and then I gave my work and direction to Janet who was still our go-to woman at Stone Lion. So, I was still working as a designer, but now I had a different relationship with the advertising firm. Now, I was the client and they were doing their best to please me.

It was wonderful being able to work and contribute without officially having a job. I did all I could to help build the Roxy's brand and help Eric with his other investments. We had talked about having children, and I already felt like I wanted to be with them as much as I could.

Eric was just happy that I could tag along with him when he traveled. He loved having me with him, and that was right where I wanted to be.

We were traveling at the moment.

We were currently in Costa Rica. There had been a fire on the farm that grew our beans. The farmers had lost two of their main structures and were scrambling to figure things out when Eric stepped in and donated the new buildings they needed. He had a good relationship with the farmers, and he didn't hesitate to help them when he heard about what happened. They had just completed the new buildings, and we flew in for the opening celebration.

We had been there for a few days already, but tonight was a party and feast before Eric and I headed back to the States. There were a few hundred people at the party, and since all of them spoke Spanish, I had been with an interpreter the whole evening.

Eric had gone off a while ago to meet some of the farm workers who would be using the new building. I could see him in the distance, smiling and shaking hands, and looking gorgeous and confident.

There was a live band and a small open area where people gathered to listen and dance. I headed that way with my interpreter whose name was Laura. I loved that she could understand me in English, and I enjoyed hanging out with her in general, so we had been talking and having fun the whole time Eric was occupied.

It was crowded near the band, so Laura and I went through the people in single-file fashion, me holding her hand as she led us to a spot near the wall. I was following her when an old withered hand reached out and touched my arm. I turned to find a little old lady, wrapped in a colorful shawl and grinning at me. Both of her front teeth were missing, but it didn't inhibit her sweet smile. It was contagious, and I smiled back at her.

Laura turned when I stopped walking and she joined me, stepping back to talk to the lady. We kind of huddled around her since the music was loud and she obviously wanted to say something. She looked directly at me as she was speaking. I held her gaze even though I couldn't understand a single word she said.

Laura had to lean in to hear her over the music. Once the lady stopped talking, I glanced at Laura for translation.

"This is Mrs. Torres," Laura said, speaking near my ear. "Her grandson is Angelo, the crop manager."

I nodded since I remembered meeting Angelo. "It's a pleasure to meet you," I said with a smile and bow.

Laura translated.

Mrs. Torres looked slowly back and forth between us and then she spoke again. She said something longer in Spanish, and I waited for her to finish and for Laura to translate.

"She says thank you. She says that her family has been working on this farm for three generations, and they have never had such a nice, uh, facilities."

"Tell her that it was our pleasure and we are so thankful we could help out."

Laura translated, and again the lady said something in Spanish. Laura smiled as she was listening and then she turned to me to translate.

"She says it makes a mother's heart happy and grateful to see her children and grandchildren looked after. She said you will know all about that soon since you and Eric are expecting a baby."

Laura shifted and stared at me, going from translator mode to her own personal reaction. "I didn't know you were going to have a baby," she added in English. "Congratulations!"

"I'm not," I said. "I mean, I want to one day, but I'm not pregnant right now. Does she think I'm pregnant?"

I wanted to reach out and touch my stomach, but I didn't let myself do it. I had eaten a lot at dinner, but I didn't think I was that bloated.

"I think she does," Laura said.

She leaned over to talk to Mrs. Torres again, Saying something in Spanish. I assumed she was informing her that I was not pregnant. The old lady nodded and patted her own tummy before saying a long sentence in Spanish to Laura.

"She said you are," Laura said, leaning in to speak to me.

I looked back and forth from her to the lady, feeling a little stunned. "Tell her I don't think I'm expecting a baby, not that I know of, and ask her what made her say that, please."

Laura spoke to the woman, who listened before speaking back to her. While they did this, I could see the lady gesturing to her own stomach and shifting her mid-section this way and that. I knew it was entirely possible that I could be pregnant, but I didn't think I was. I hadn't even missed a period yet. I was supposed to start in the next couple of days. Laura leaned over to speak to me after conversing with the lady.

"She says she can tell you are by your posture, the way you carry yourself. She says you guard yourself, you know, your middle, when you move around. She says you will be a beautiful, caring mother with how you're already guarding that baby."

Tears sprang to my eyes, because it felt in my heart that what she was saying was the truth. Even if I wasn't pregnant yet, I knew I would guard Eric's baby with my life.

I took a test when we made it home the following day, and it came out negative.

I passed it off as an odd conversation with a curious old lady.

But then, five days later, once I was officially late for my period, I took another test which came out positive. It just goes to show you that old Costa Rican ladies are sometimes more accurate than a pregnancy test.

Even after I gave birth to Eden Rose the following May, I never forgot that lady who told me I was expecting her and that I would be a great mom.

I eventually painted her from memory. It wasn't an exact likeness, but I painted her from a distance, and I definitely captured her essence. That painting hung in the roasting house for a year until someone from the farm saw it in a photo and had to have it.

Roxy's got a lot of free coffee as a trade for that deal. The coffee farm was flourishing, and they were looking for a way to repay our kindness anyway, so they way-overpaid in trade. The best part was that the painting was now cherished in the home of the woman's grandson.

In the years that followed, I made a lot of art. Sometimes I'd draw, and sometimes I'd paint, and sometimes I'd design digitally. Sometimes I depicted people and situations I knew deeply like my two daughters, or my mother, or my home, or our racehorses, and others were of people like Mrs. Torres who I had barely crossed paths with.

But most of my art was inspired by one person. The answer to my brother's prayer, and ultimately the answer to mine. My muse, my friend, my lover, my partner, my protector, my helper, my man, my husband. Eric. My happily ever after.

The End
(till book 5)

Thanks to my team ~ Chris, Coda, Jan, Glenda, and Yvette